The Stolen Sky
and other strange tales

by
B.J. West

apocryphile press
BERKELEY, CA

Apocryphile Press
1700 Shattuck Ave #81
Berkeley, CA 94709
www.apocryphile.org

Printed in the United States of America
ISBN 9781940671734

Table of Contents

The Stolen Sky 5

The Put-pocket.. 29

Braid 35

Stroke of Luck... 75

Homecoming.. 77

Altruism 91

Conjunction of Solitude 97

No Deposit, No Return... 107

A Distant Baying.. 111

Souvenirs 123

Whispers and Frost 137

One

The Stolen Sky

Lying on his back, deep in the tall grass on the edge of the field, Blair Larson stared up at the sky. He was watching the falcon soaring above him so intently that he didn't notice the approaching footsteps until a pair of boots nearly touched the top of his head.

"You OK?"

He sat up and found himself facing an old Native American man with dark skin dried and wrinkled by many years of sun and dust, and long gray hair cascading around his shoulders. He would never have guessed the old man was a falconer if not for the kestrel standing unhooded on his glove. The Indian clutched a can of beer in the other hand, as if to balance the bird's weight.

"I almost stepped on you," the man said before taking a swallow from the beer. He looked Blair over for a moment. "Where's your bird?"

"Oh, I'm not a falconer," Blair said, clambering to his feet and extending his hand. "I'm a vet. Blair Larson."

The man made no attempt to empty a hand for shaking. "You're that bird doctor."

Blair smiled. "Yeah, that's me."

The old man stared at Blair for what seemed like a long time, then nodded as if he had arrived at some conclusion. "I'm Joseph Littledeer. You want a beer?" Without waiting for an answer, he turned and walked away. Intrigued, Blair trotted behind.

Without saying another word, Joseph led him to a battered, ancient pickup truck parked apart from most of the other cars on the edge of the field where the falconry meet was being held. When he got there, Joseph tossed his empty can into a pile of others in the bed of the truck, then reached into an equally crusty old cooler, pulled out a can, and tossed it to Blair. Through it all, the falcon sitting on his glove remained perfectly calm. Normally, a falconer would hood their bird, as falcons are notoriously skittish among unexpected noises and unfamiliar movements. Joseph's falcon, however, just watched with disinterest as its master opened another beer for himself and walked away.

Blair followed along as Joseph made his way over to a small hillside overlooking the hunting field. Joseph sat down in the tall grass, and Blair did likewise. They sat in silence, watching the current competitor fly. Blair quickly forgot about his strange companion as he became absorbed in the hunt. He didn't watch the gloved man flushing the prey. Instead, he gazed at the beautiful Peregrine circling the field and waiting. In moments, a pheasant lunged out of its hiding place, and the falcon fell out of the sky like a stone. It snatched its prey aloft, breaking its spine in one savage, poetic arc. Blair suddenly realized that his heartbeat was racing and his breathing had become rapid.

And that the old man was watching him. "You were flying," he said.

Blair laughed, a bit embarrassed. "Yeah, I guess I was."

Joseph nodded, and returned his gaze to the competition. A woman launched her Harris hawk, then began tramping around in the brush, trying to flush out a jackrabbit. Without looking away, he said "I think the falcon is your totem animal."

Blair raised an eyebrow. "My what?"

"Everyone has an animal they resonate with. It acts out their inner nature. Its spirit lives within them."

"Oh," said Blair. "Like when you say someone is a dog person or a cat person?"

"Yeah. Except those would be pretty boring people. There are wolf people, and trout people, those who laugh with the spirit of the otter, and those who are treacherous like the blue jay." He tipped back the last of his beer. "Yours is definitely the falcon."

"I guess that makes sense." Blair shrugged. "I've always loved birds. Their elegance, their cruelty. There's nothing more amazing than a raptor in flight. I mean, that's exactly why I became an avian specialist in the first place.

Joseph nodded knowingly. "Maybe you can help Dolores."

"Dolores?"

"Yeah." He gestured with his gloved hand. "She's lost the will to fly."

Blair looked at the kestrel. Aside from being unnaturally calm, there didn't appear to be anything unusual about it. "She can't fly?"

"I think she *can* fly, but she *won't*." He raised and dropped his arm suddenly, holding tightly to the jesses securing the bird's legs. She flapped her wings violently, then settled back into her stoic stance.

"Well, her wing motion looks normal enough, but there's no way I could tell you anything out here. Why don't you bring her into the clinic and I'll give her a proper exam?"

"Hmmm." Joseph looked at his falcon. "I don't have much money."

"That's okay. I won't charge you for the exam, and I'm sure we can make arrangements about any treatment she might need." Blair took out a business card, then reached over and slipped it into Joseph's shirt pocket. The gesture seemed more intimate than it should have.

* * *

Susan Coe had just entered the clinic, draping her purse and jacket over the back of her chair when her phone rang. Glancing at the caller ID, she sat her cup of coffee on her desk and answered. "Hey, Blair."

"Hey Susan. Could you come to my office when you get a second?"

She was about to answer "sure thing" when she realized he'd hung up on her. Despite being a licenced veterinary surgeon and a full partner at the clinic, Blair always treated her like a glorified vet tech, which was infuriating.

Blair was busy typing when she rapped on his doorframe. He glanced up for a moment, then returned his eyes to the monitor. "Got a research assignment for you today." His fingers continued tapping on the keyboard. "What's our schedule look like?"

"We've got the papillectomy on Mrs. Dupree's cockatoo at eleven, the condor with aspergillosis at two, and don't forget that owl from San Diego that swallowed a key."

Dr. Larson's fingers halted as he weighed his options. "Okay, I need you for the condor, but I can handle the cockatoo alone. Until then I need you to find anything you can related to the work of Dr. Perry L. Greenberg. Journal articles, press clippings, anything. And I'll need his office number. I'm going to want to talk to him."

Susan raised her eyebrows. "Care to at least tell me what kind of doctor he is?"

"Neurosurgeon. Saw him on TV last night. He's doing some amazing things with direct interface between a human nervous system and a computer. He can pull sensory data from one person's brain and send it to someone else's brain. It's called "ghosting.""

"Ghosting?"

"Yeah, everything the first person sees, hears, smells or feels is sent to the second person, and they experience it just as if it were happening to them. They've mostly been using it for law enforcement. The supreme court just heard a case where an informant was being ghosted in a narcotics sting. The informant was killed, but they ruled that the cop who was ghosting him could testify as if he had been present when it happened, even though he was *physically* several blocks away in a hotel room."

"Neat." Susan sipped at her coffee. "So what's that got to do with us?"

Blair's eyes flitted momentarily towards the window. "I'm not sure yet. He's breaking all kinds of ground in neural microsurgery. I have a feeling his techniques might be useful."

She shrugged. "OK, I'm on it." And since he seemed to be completely lost in his work again, Susan drifted back to her office. "Great," she muttered. "I'm back to being a research assistant."

*　*　*

Terry Weinman fumbled her keys to the clinic's front door, and was shocked to find it unlocked. She was normally the first person there, and was responsible for turning on all the lights and starting the first pot of coffee. This morning, all the lights were already on, and the acrid reek of a coffee pot boiled dry filled the room. She dashed to the kitchen and slapped the coffee maker's power switch off, muttering with disgust at the bubbled black carbon on the bottom of the glass carafe.

And then she heard the screaming.

At first, she thought it was a woman, or maybe a child. And it was coming from the surgery room.

Her heart pounding, she dashed through the doors, staring for several seconds until she could comprehend the scene before her. Dr. Larson was operating the controls of the microsurgical robot, his face buried in the hooded eyepieces. A seagull was strapped to the operating table, wings spread and immobilized, its spine opened like a book, exposing the vertebrae. The robot's probes were imbedded into the tangled skein of nerves at the base of the neck, quivering slightly. The gull struggled against the clamps pinning it to the table and screeched horribly.

"Dr. Larson?"

Blair looked up from the instruments. "Terry? What are you doing here?"

"Uh, I heard the screaming…" She couldn't tear her eyes from the bird's exposed spine.

"Is it morning already?" He glanced at his watch.

"Uh, yeah. Dr. Larson? Shouldn't that bird be, uh, knocked out?"

Blair blinked against the dim light of the room. "Can't. I'm charting the signal output in individual nerve strands. If it was unconscious, there wouldn't be any signal. I've pretty much got the whole visual cortex mapped out…." Then he finally noticed her horrified expression. "Oh! Don't worry! It's under a local, it's not feeling any pain."

"Then why is it screaming like that?"

"It's just irritated about being held down. Gulls are noisy birds anyway. I wish I'd thought to bring in some ear plugs."

He rubbed his eyes, and Terry thought he looked rather haggard. "You been here all night?"

"Yeah, I guess so. Could you bring me a cup of coffee?"

Reminded of the crusted mess left in the carafe, she was finally able to look away from the flayed seagull. She opened her mouth to protest, but Dr. Larson had already buried his face back into the machine.

* * *

Blair laid on his sofa, fidgeting. His doctor's post surgery instructions were clear; stay home, take it easy, keep the lights down low, no reading or television, no loud music, lay down as much as possible. He'd lasted exactly two days before he started breaking the rules.

At first, he limited his reading to no more than ten minutes a day, after that he'd develop a throbbing headache that no amount of vicodin could defeat. He could barely make out the letters on the page, wandering through a field of soft word-shaped blobs hunting for meaning. He became accustomed to the pain, squinted until he could read, and was soon spending most of the day doing more research.

By the fourth day he was pacing. He peeled off the bandages on the back of his head, following the stubble where he'd been shaved to the cold metal of the implant. His scalp felt raw and battered, but he ignored the pain, gently tracing a circle around the jack.

He'd been warned by Dr. Greenberg not to try out the interface for another two months and even then only after an extensive battery of tests, but was becoming increasingly apparent – at least to Blair – that that was completely unacceptable. He *had* to know.

Driving was also off limits, but Blair could wait no longer. He gently lowered himself into the driver's seat, pulled the door closed after him while being careful not to turn his head. He felt dizzy, so he rested a moment to let it pass before starting the car. He backed slowly out of his driveway, pausing as a passing car honked at him, then sped off down the road towards the clinic.

He began having doubts about the wisdom of driving very quickly. Every turn set his inner ears whirling, and his vision was doubling badly. His depth perception was off, and he narrowly missed being t-boned by a truck he thought was farther away than it really was. By the time he pulled into the parking lot, he was exhausted and his shirt was damp with sweat. He sat panting for several moments before slowly easing out of the car and shuffling into the building.

"Dr. Larson!" Terry shouted, surprised as he entered the clinic. Her shrill voice stabbed at his ears. "I thought you weren't coming back for another month."

He forced a smile. "Oh, I'm not back. I just have to pick up some things I need at home." He hurried past her, eager to avoid further conversation.

He went straight to the cage where his last experimental patient was perched. It had survived the procedure, and was recovering very strongly. It was clearly unhappy with the bandages around its neck and the small box harnessed on its back between its wings, fidgeting and rocking back and forth on its perch while looking around with bright, alert eyes.

He chuckled, rubbing his bandages softly. "Believe me, big guy, I know just how you feel." With growing excitement, Blair put on gloves and reached into the cage. The gull managed a ginger peck on the glove, but it must have hurt, as it didn't try it again. Blair gently switched on the transmitter and returned the bird to its cage.

The receiving unit was about the size of a pack of cigarettes, and Blair stuck it in his smock pocket, unreeling the cord. He carefully inserted the microplug into the socket on the back of his neck, expecting it to hurt, but surprised that it didn't. He kept his fingers on it, ready to yank it out again if neccissary. With a little trepidation, he touched the power button on the receiver.

Suddenly, he was across the room, looking out from between bars. His head darted around quickly, seeing everything in crystalline focus. The muscles in his neck stabbed with pain each time he moved his head. Blair wondered for a split second if there was some kind of feedback in the muscular signal, and with a rush of glee realized that it was just residual pain from the bird's surgery. He was ghosting the gull, seeing out of its eyes as though they were his own!

With ears more sensitive than he had ever thought possible, he heard someone laugh, a loud, crude sound. With instincts he could not ignore, he whipped around to see the source of the sound, and was a little surprised to find a man staring at him, one hand covering his mouth as if to hide the child-like smile. That's *me*, Blair thought. Startled to see himself, he opened his eyes...

The gull was in his line of sight, staring directly at him. He saw himself through the bird's eyes, and the bird through his own, *and the bird was seeing him and itself through his eyes, and he was looking at the bird who was looking at him who was looking at the bird who was looking at him who was looking...*

He yanked the cord out of the socket in his neck, reeling at the sudden plunge back into his own throbbing head. The gull screeched and beat its wings in protest at the intrusion.

* * *

Blair leaped out of the truck and immediately put on his gloves. Michael Cowell, the clinic's anesthesiologist, came around the other side and began opening the back of the truck.

"Dr. Larson, are you sure this is a good idea?"

Blair smiled. "You'd rather be at work than on the beach?"

Michael ignored the joke. "What if something goes wrong? We're at least an hour from the nearest hospital."

"Relax, Michael. Nothing'll go wrong." He opened the cage and carefully lifted the struggling seagull out with both hands. The gleaming plugs nestled under the bird's downy feathers had healed as perfectly as his had. He switched on the bird's transmitter.

"You have the mask?"

Michael pulled a fur lined sleep mask out of his jacket.

"Put it on me, then switch on my receiver."

Michael hesitated. "You *do* know you won't be getting this bird back, right?"

"Yes, Michael."

"OK." He slipped the mask over Blair's eyes. "Kinky," he muttered as he pressed the button on the black box clipped to Blair's belt.

The seagull blinked against the brilliant sunlight, and the realization that it was outdoors at the ocean surged through it. With a slight chuckle, Blair focused enough to hurl the bird upward.

With a beating of mighty wings, the gull soared aloft, gaining altitude with every flap. Blair was dimly aware that somewhere below he reeled and fell, his assistant catching him and easing him to the ground. None of that mattered. He was *flying*.

It was harder work than he'd expected. Muscles that Blair knew so well from the outside were now working together as they were meant to. Parts of the brain that were used for no other purpose took stock of the wind conditions, and worked to harness them.

The gull spiraled in an updraft, with barely a glance down to the tiny specs on the beach that had been its captors only moments ago.

Blair thrilled at his vantage point, the beach a golden ribbon of sand stretching out to the horizon in opposite directions, dividing the land from the infinite sapphire ocean. The gull flexed its wings slightly, reaching for enough lift to climb above an approaching flock of pelicans flying in a ragged wedge formation. Hundreds of feet up, the gull found a crosswind and eased into it, effortlessly surfing the eddies and currents of this invisible river in the sky. It carried him swiftly out to sea, where it spied the jewel-like colors of a coral reef just below the water's surface. The gull stretched and dropped out of the slipstream, heading toward the reef, where it knew it would find food...

Blair's mind plunged into darkness as the images and sensations broke up. The gull had flown beyond the range of the transmitter, leaving Blair once again alone in his body. The feeling of being stranded on the ground, like a bit of driftwood washed up on the shore overwhelmed him. He whipped off the mask, blinking in the harsh sunlight. He stared in the direction the bird had gone, trying to find a spec against the blue horizon, but his eyes suddenly seemed woefully inadequate.

"You okay, Dr. Larson?"

Blair gave up searching for the gull and squinted at Michael. "Yeah, I'm fine."

"Then how come you're crying?"

He reached up and touched his face, which was wet, and smiled. "Because that was the most incredible experience I've ever had in my life."

"It worked then?"

He barked a laugh. "Oh yeah, I think you could say it worked. The only down side was that I was just a passenger. I had no way of getting the gull to go where I wanted it to, or even to look in any specific direction." His mind was already back at the clinic, pouring over modifications to his system.

* * *

"Mr. Littledeer?" Blair cradled the phone to his ear, glad to be alone in his office. He felt as nervous as a school boy getting up the nerve to talk to his crush.

"Hi Doc. What's up? You need to see Dolores again?"

Blair fidgeted in his chair. "No, no, nothing like that. I... I'd like your help with something."

"My help? What can I do for you?"

"I'd like to take up falconry."

Much to Blair's surprise, the old man laughed. "No you wouldn't. Trust me."

"No, really, I would."

"You willing to give up your life for it? Cause that's what it takes."

"What do you mean?"

The old man sighed. "I know you handle birds all the time, so you know how dangerous they can be. Well that never goes away. You can't tame a falcon, *ever*. A falcon isn't a pet, it becomes your master. It doesn't matter if you're tired, or sick, or if the weather is miserable. You have to attend to it night and day with a devotion most reserve for their spouses. You married Dr. Larson?"

Blair chuckled. "Never found a woman who could stand to live with me."

"That's good. Most falconers' marriages don't last long." He didn't sound like he was joking. "You ready to give up your yard? You're gonna have to build mews to keep the bird in, and get them inspected."

"I've converted my garage to mews and they've already been approved by Fish and Game."

That stopped him for a moment. "Oh, you really are serious."

"More than I can tell you," Blair said solemnly. "I know all about the licensing process, and I'm ready to take the test. The only thing I need now is a sponsor." He took a deep breath. "Mr. Littledeer, would you take me on as your apprentice?" There, he'd said it. Blair squirmed as the silence on the line seemed to stretch out for hours.

"Okay," came the reply at long last. "I guess if anyone can take care of a bird, it's you. And I owe you for letting Dolores fly again."

Blair hadn't been aware that he'd been holding his breath until he finally released it. "Thank you, Joseph. Can I come by tomorrow with the papers?"

* * *

As an apprentice, the only birds Blair could legally start with were a kestrel or a red tail hawk. Despite Joseph's adamant recommendation that he start with the easier to train kestrel, Blair chose the faster, shorter winged hawk. He bought an immature tiercel red tail, which he named Mariah.

Not wishing to interfere with the bird's development, Blair decided not to implant the interface until it was fully grown, which meant waiting nearly a year. He spent that year taking Mariah out to hunt the old-fashioned way, often accompanied by Joseph Littledeer and

Dolores. He enjoyed learning the ancient sport, but always found something deeply unsatisfying in standing around waiting as his bird flew, like watching somebody else eat cake.

When Mariah was finally mature enough for the operation, Blair fitted the hawk with his latest interface design, then resigned himself to waiting until the plugs had fully healed. It was hard being patient. He remembered what it had been like as a kid, counting down the seconds until Christmas morning. But this time he wasn't working with a common seagull. Hawks were protected, and if something went wrong, the resulting brouhaha would no doubt attract the attention of the animal rights people.

Finally, the waiting was over. In the safety of his home office, he turned on the caged bird's transceiver, masked himself, then activated his own. At first, Mariah barely noticed the arrival of his unseen companion. That all changed when Blair flipped the switch on his override.

Panic gripped the hawk as Blair seized active control of its body, forcing its consciousness into the background. Suddenly, Blair *was* the bird, not merely feeling what it felt, but wearing its skin as if it were his own. He looked around, finding his masked self perched on a stool nearby. Cautiously, Blair flexed a wing, extending it delicately, splaying the feathers on the tip. Motion caught his eye, and he realized that his human body was holding its arm out as well. He raised both wings, both arms raising identically. He dropped them and focused on raising the bird's wings without moving his real body. It took a lot of focus and practice, but eventually he was able to control the bird while remaining fairly still, save small twitches of his fingers.

He thumbed the transceiver off and was flung out of the bird and back into his own body, feeling as though he had actually crossed the physical distance in between, but knowing it was just an illusion.

The room erupted with screeching. Blair ripped off his mask to find Mariah flailing her wings against her cage, shaking her head violently and crying in protest. Satisfied that she was back in control of her own body, the hawk began to settle down, pacing back and forth on her perch. Blair smiled. Eventually, the bird would get used to being possessed.

* * *

"Look, Mr. Gilbert," Susan spat furiously into the phone. She rarely actually talked to the clients, but the man from the Department of the Interior had verbally battered Terry to the point of tears, and Susan had no choice but to intervene. "I am perfectly aware that the bald eagle is an endangered species. I also know that it's the national symbol. Yes, I'm sure it is an emergency. None of this is going to make Dr. Larson *magically* appear just because you want him to. As Terry already tried to tell you, we will have Dr. Larson call you the moment he comes in."

She desperately wished that it had been Mr. Gilbert who had tangled with some power lines in Alaska instead of an innocent national treasure. "We'll keep paging Dr. Larson. We'll keep leaving messages for him at home. When we finally reach him, we will tell him about your situation, and he will no doubt call you back promptly. When he does, I suggest that you find the restraint to be more civil than you've been with me, or you may just have to make do with the staff that you already have."

She slammed the phone down, seething. "Where. Is. He?"

Terry winced. "He's flying." She added air quotes around the last word.

Susan grimaced. She had gone with him on one of his outings. At first, she'd been repelled by the sight of her blindfolded boss slouched on the ground twitching, but that quickly gave way to being bored of hanging around waiting for him to finish. She never went with him again.

Even worse, this obsession with his new hobby was causing Blair to neglect his practice. She had to pickup the slack, carrying a larger workload, delving into more complex procedures than her veterinary license technically allowed for. People came to the clinic because they wanted the famous Dr. Blair Larson to save their birds. The scandal that would break if people knew how many operations were being done by his underlings while he was off playing in a field would no doubt kill the practice in a heartbeat. She wasn't sure how much longer she could cover for Blair. She wasn't sure how much longer she was willing to.

* * *

"I think you're going to like this," Blair said as he pulled the truck to a stop by the edge of the field. Joseph Littledeer shrugged, causing Dolores to shift slightly on his glove. Blair dropped the tailgate of the pickup, opened the door to the cage and stepped aside. Mariah immediately scrambled into desperate, panicked flight.

Joseph gasped as Blair made no attempt to restrain her, didn't even watch where she flew. "You let her go!"

Blair smiled. "Don't worry, I'll catch up with her in a second."

Joseph watched confused as Blair sat down in the shade of the truck, leaned back against the rear tire, and adjusted the mask into place. Blair had been a bit nervous the first few times he'd done this alone, leaving himself vulnerable to anyone who might wander along. But then he imagined any would-be assailant's surprise when a hawk dropped out of the sky, talons ripping into them, sending them fleeing from their unconscious victim's supernatural defender. He smiled securely as he felt for the receiver tucked into his shirt pocket, plugged its cord into his neck socket, and turned it on.

Joseph craned his neck back and shielded his eyes from the sun, trying to keep an eye on Mariah as she circled overhead. The moment Blair touched the box in his pocket, the hawk shrieked and plummeted from the sky. She recovered just before hitting the ground, then flew directly to Blair's outstretched glove.

"What did you just do?" Joseph murmured, staring at the tiny box nestled between the bird's shoulders.

"I just *became* the bird," Blair slurred. Mariah looked Joseph directly in the eye, slowly stretched out a wing and waved, as a human might. Joseph stared with his mouth agape, and nearly jumped out of his skin when Blair suddenly launched the red-tail back into the air.

"She's hungry," muttered Blair. It was spring, and high above the field he could see it was practically crawling with young jack rabbits. Effortlessly, he snatched one off the ground, killed it, and settled onto a large, hot rock. He ripped the fur off with his beak, gorging himself on the glistening pink meat. He had come to appreciate the flavor of the eyes, and usually saved them for last. When there was nothing left but a bloody pile of fur and bones, he took off again.

The hunger remained. The rabbit had been rather small, so he allowed himself another. It took effort to choke down the last few bites, and he left a considerable amount of meat on the carcass. Several crows hovered nearby, jealously eying the remains and already jockeying with each other for position. Blair still felt hungry, and at last realized that it wasn't Mariah that needed to eat, it was *him*.

The crows landed before Blair had even flapped his wings twice, greedily tearing at the leavings. Once again, he grabbed some altitude, then swooped down upon another ill-fated rabbit. He yanked it aloft, and quickly flew the distance back to the truck. He landed at the feet of the man leaning against the rear wheel.

He was seized with an instinctive fear that the man might suddenly awake and lash out at him, but he forced himself to remember that he was looking at himself through borrowed eyes. He wrestled the fear down, hopped closer, and dropped the bloody rabbit into his own lap. He smiled, and thought it odd how strange it was to look up at teeth made for chewing plants, surrounded by loose flesh adorned with a dusting of scrubby hair. He flapped back up onto the tailgate, then hopped into the cage. Now came the hard part.

Blair concentrated on his human body, first flexing fingers, then stretching his arms. He blindly got up off the ground, being careful not to let the rabbit drop onto the dirt. Watching himself from a removed perspective, he guided his clumsy hands to the cage door, closing and latching it. He then thumbed the unit in his pocket and was plunged into darkness.

Sunlight stabbed at his eyes as he removed his blindfold. He blinked a few times, then focused enough to find the ashen face of Joseph Littledeer.

"My God, what have you done?" He was shaking and Dolores thrashed wildly on his glove.

"I've learned to fly! Isn't it amazing?"

"No, it's horrible!"

"What?" Blair stammered. "I thought if anyone could appreciate what I've done…"

"What you've done is a crime against nature." He stopped struggling with his falcon long enough to point at Mariah who was also screaming and flailing in his cage. "You're raping one of the most noble creatures on Earth."

Blair squinted at the back of the truck. "Oh, don't worry about her, she'll settle down in a few minutes."

Tears were running down Joseph's wrinkled face as he took a hood from his pocket and wrestled it on to Dolores's head. She settled down slightly, but was still clearly agitated. Joseph turned his back to Blair, head hung low. "You are trying to steal the sky. I'm sorry I helped you."

"You don't understand. I'm not hurting her, I just…"

Joseph began walking away down the gravel road.

"Hey! Where are you going? Don't you want a ride back into town?"

He kept walking without response.

Blair was suddenly furious. "Fine! Walk home then! Who the hell are you to judge me? What I've done is a fucking *miracle!*" He glared at Joseph's back, baffled at how the old man could fail to appreciate what he'd accomplished. "I'm not going to be gravity's bitch anymore."

His knotted stomach churned, reminding him of his hunger. Dismissing the old man from his mind, he perched on the edge of the tailgate, took out his knife and gutted the rabbit, then lost himself in a feast of raw meat for the third time.

* * *

Susan and Michael glanced at each other, stunned. Without a word, Blair had stepped away from the unconscious bald eagle spread out on the surgical table, and wandered over to the window.

"Would you look at those cumulus clouds? Those are some *serious* updrafts. I bet they go up at least six thousand feet."

"Doctor Larson?" Concern flooded Michael's tone. "I'm not sure how much longer I can safely keep the anesthesia going."

With great effort, Blair tore his eyes away from the sky, and followed Susan's furious glare down to the motionless raptor, its leg and side still splayed wide open. "Right." He muttered as he stepped back to the table. He picked up his scalpel, but only held it motionless.

"Damn it Blair," Susan spat. "You've got to *focus*. This isn't some stupid canary here. You fuck this up and you're done."

"Yeah," Blair said, rubbing his eyes. "Maybe you're right." And with that he sat the scalpel back on the table and started removing his gloves.

"What are you're doing? I can't finish this without you."

"Sure you can." Blair pulled off his disposable smock, dropped it on the floor and started to leave the room.

Susan stepped in between him and the door. "You walk away from this and I won't cover for you any more. I mean it, Blair. You're walking away from me, from the clinic, from your license, *everything*."

He nodded. "Like you said. I'm done." He glanced at the window again, then stared impatiently at Susan.

Reeling with rage and disbelief, she shrugged and stepped aside, allowing Blair to move past her and through the swinging doors.

* * *

Blair had been flying nearly constantly in the weeks since he'd freed himself of the distractions of the clinic. His face was now swaddled in a scruffy beard, and his muscles ached from lack of exercise. Neither of these things concerned him. He'd begun thinking of his earth-bound body as a necessary nuisance, something to be maintained only as much as he had to in the times between flying sessions.

As he returned home, he was surprised to find a small fleet of cars around his house, several police cars taking up his driveway. He pulled the truck as close as he could, and got out. The sheriff met him at the door, looking quite tense. "Blair Larson? These men are from Animal Control. I have a warrant for the confiscation of any birds on the premise."

Blair blinked. "There must be a mistake. They took my veterinary license, not my falconry license."

"Well, sir, as of this morning, your property has been seized as part of the civil and criminal actions against you. You will be allowed to gather some things, and then you have to go."

Panic seized him as he began to realize the full gravity of the situation. "But my birds..."

"I'm sorry, Dr. Larson."

One of the animal control people was wearing thick leather gloves and face protection, and opening the cage in the back of the pickup.

"Hey! Get away from there!" Blair shouted and started to run towards him, but the Sheriff grabbed him by his elbow.

"Dr. Larson, this will go much easier if you just cooperate."

"You can't have Mariah! You don't understand! She's *different*! She's a *part of me*!" Blair squirmed free of the Sheriff's grip, and hurled himself at the animal handler. The man had Mariah half out of the cage when Blair tackled him, scratching with his hands like an animal. Caught off guard, he dropped the hawk, which immediately took off toward the horizon.

The Sheriff pulled Blair off of the shaken man, slammed him face down into the gravel and dust, wrestled his arms behind him and slapped handcuffs around his wrists. Two of the Sherrif's men wrestled him into the back of the patrol carand slammed the door. Blair screamed and thrashed around wildly as they drove off.

"Mr. Larsen, if you don't calm down, we're gonna have to reclassify you as 51-50, and you'll be spending a long time in the looney bin instead of just sitting in a cell overnight. Is that what you want?"

Blair didn't cease his hysterics, giving no sign at all that he'd even heard the Sheriff. He was equally unresponsive as the Sheriff radioed in their change in destination.

It took three burly orderlies to extract Blair from the car and wrestle him into a straight jacket. The Sheriff said "good luck with that," gave a little salute and left as quickly as he could.

They dragged Blair in and held him as the doctor gave him an injection of sedatives. Once he started to settle down, they ushered Blair into his cell, easing him down onto the heavily padded cot.

Blair never uttered a single intelligible word through the whole struggle, but as chemical unconsciousness settled onto him, he summoned the last of his strength for a final ear-piercing screech.

* * *

Mariah soared as high as she could, putting distance between herself and the humans that had been scuffling on the ground. She'd become a little unaccustomed to flying of her own volition, but regained comfort with it very quickly. The air currents were comforting, and for a while she merely darted about, reveling in her ability to choose for herself where to go. Before long, she forgot that it was ever an issue.

Movement in the grass below caught her eye, and before she had even become consciously aware that it was a mole, she was plummeting towards it, talons raised for the kill.

As she dove, Mariah could already see the kill happening in her mind. She knew precisely how her talons were about to puncture the mole's hide, biting into its flesh, the impact slamming the breath out of its lungs, whipping its head to the side with vertebrae snapping force. And in some unfamiliar way, Mariah understood how much this death was going to hurt her prey. She could feel the pain that the rodent was about to experience, almost as though *she* were the mole and it was happening to her.

Confused by these strange thoughts and feelings, Mariah flinched, retracting her talons at the last possible second and missing the mole by a hair's breadth. The mole, suddenly panicked to realize that it was being hunted, darted down its hole unharmed.

Something deep and new in Mariah was pleased, knowing that she had been merciful.

And for the first time in her life, the hawk was gripped by the icy chill of fear.

Two

The Put-pocket

I was only in New York for the night, stranded between business meetings. I had originally planned on killing the evening with a show, but somehow I just couldn't bring myself to drop $200 watching grown adults act out a Disney cartoon I wasn't that hot on anyway.

Still, it was too early to go back to the hotel, so I wandered around randomly until I bungled my way into a sports bar on a side street. The place was mostly empty, just a handful of fellow refugees looking for a cold drink and a game to distract themselves with.

The Phillies were starting to recover from a disastrous third inning when he came in. He exchanged nods of recognition with the bartender, then walked past a long line of empty stools to perch on the one next to mine. "Who's winning?" he muttered as the bartender sat a beer in front of him.

"The Mets, by four," I croaked, my voice sounding somehow unfamiliar.

We stared at the TV silently for a while, until peripherally I noticed that the newcomer was starting at me. He smiled when I turned to face him. "You here on business?"

I nodded. "You?"

"Nah, I live here, NYC born and raised!" he took a sip of his beer, then looked me over again. "You're from California." It wasn't a question.

"Yeah, how can you tell?"

"I've got a knack. Los Angeles?"

I smiled, impressed. "Close, San Fernando. What gives it away?"

He laughed. "Your driver's license."

Startled, I slapped my hand to my back pocket. My wallet was still there. The kid just grinned at me, clearly enjoying my discomfort. Determined to be a good sport, I smiled back. "Heh, you really had me going for a second there."

"Don't worry. I'm not a thief. I'm a putpocket."

"You're a what now?"

"A putpocket."

"Don't you mean a *pick*pocket?"

He looked a little annoyed. "If I'd meant a pickpocket, I'd have said a pickpocket."

I was beginning to suspect that the kid might be crazy. He certainly looked the part, old army surplus jacket, knit watch cap over stringy, unwashed hair. I put his age around twenty-five, but the patina of street life made him look older.

I tried to ignore him, focusing more intently on the game than it really warranted. At first it looked like it would work, the kid content to doodle on a napkin. But when he finished his drawing, he slid it across the bar in front of me. He'd drawn a crude cartoon of a crab wearing a Yankees baseball cap.

I pushed the cartoon back. "Don't quit your day job."

"I only work at night," he smirked, taking the drawing back and putting it in his pocket. He sat back and crossed his arms, so obviously waiting for me to ask that I obliged him.

"OK, you've got me. What does a *putpocket* do?"

"Pretty much what you'd think. I put stuff in people's pockets."

"What kind of stuff?"

He shrugged. "Whatever someone wants me to put there. Lately it's been a lot of flyers and business cards, y'know? Advertising shit."

I raised an eyebrow. "Someone pays you for that?"

"You'd be surprised. Any mook can hand out flyers on the corner, but most people'll chuck 'em without even looking at them." He motioned the bartender over for another beer. "But if you find that same flyer in your own pocket, you'll take a good look at it, maybe even try to remember why you kept it in the first place." He grinned. "There *must* have been a reason, or you wouldn't have pocketed it, right?"

I stared at him, trying to figure out if he was yanking my chain. I decided it was easier to just go with it. "Make good money?"

"Eh. The ad jobs help pay the bills, but mostly it just keeps me in practice for plants. That's where the real money is."

"Plants," I muttered, trying to imagine him sneaking a fern into someone's purse.

"Yeah. Let's say you're a cop, and you want to take down some perp, but you ain't been able to get anything on him. You get something like a dime bag of coke, give it to me, and I put it on him just before you bust him in front of the fuckin' Mayor or something. Your stooge screams bloody murder that the dope ain't his, but can't figure out how the hell it got there."

A chill ran up my spine. "You plant evidence for the cops…"

"Not just the cops, anyone that can pay. I had this one guy who hired me to get a girl. She wouldn't go out with him because she already had a boyfriend. He figures if the boyfriend is gone, he's got a chance at her, so he hires me to slip a picture of some hot broad into his wallet, and it's got a phone number and a love note written on the back. Sure enough, she finds it before he does and kicks his ass out."

Now I was sure he was lying. "So your guy gets the girl?"

"Nah, she wasn't into him anyway, she'd just been using the boyfriend as an excuse."

"Doesn't sound like a satisfied customer."

He held up his hands. "Hey, I can't promise that some hair-brained scheme is gonna work. I just guarantee that the package will be delivered without the shill knowing."

"That's gotta be almost impossible," I smirked.

"Some jobs are harder than others. You just want a flyer in someone's purse or back pocket? I can do that shit in my sleep. You want a business card in someone's wallet? That's gonna cost you, cause first I have to lift the wallet, stay close while I plant the package, then I have to put it back, all without being caught."

"So why not just keep the wallet once you have it?"

The kid snarled. "Because I'm not a god-damned thief!"

"Right, sorry, you already told me that."

He settled down. "Besides, any schlub can pick pockets. What *I* do is a fucking art form." The pride in his voice seemed genuine. "Besides, the money I'm making is way better than the chump change people carry around in their pockets."

The TV roared as Martinez hit a high-flying triple. My companion looked up at the screen with a startled expression, but it wasn't the game that had grabbed his interest. "Oh, Christ, look at the time! You wouldn't be going to the airport tonight, wouldja?"

"No, sorry. I'm here through tomorrow."

"That's too bad. I've got a plane to catch. I've got a job in D.C." He rummaged around in his dirty, battered coat and fished out an equally battered wallet. He winked at me as he set some money down on the bar. "Watch the news for the next couple of days."

And just as suddenly as he'd appeared, the kid vanished through the door. I shook my head. I'd heard of Manhattan's reputation as a kook magnet, now I knew that it was earned.

I turned my attention to the remainder of the game, finishing my beer as the Phillies failed to turn things around fast enough to matter. As the announcer began droning his final analysis, I waved the bartender over to settle up. The damage wasn't bad enough to use the credit card, so I opened my wallet for some cash.

Only there wasn't any.

Where I'd once had at least fifty dollars was a napkin, on which was drawn a cartoon crab wearing a Yankee's cap. Only now, in a little word balloon, he was saying "In your shirt pocket."

I felt under my sport coat, and sure enough, there was a wad of bills tucked into my shirt.

He was good, but as he said, he wasn't a thief.

As I paid the bartender and stepped out into the chill of a New York night, I found myself feeling oddly sorry for some hapless senator.

Three

Braid

It was a beautiful day, the sun shining beatifically down from a cloudless sky. It was warm, but a gentle breeze kept it from being too hot. Fifteen-year-old Joshua Webster was walking home from high school, whistling a happy little tune. Birds were singing in the trees, almost as if trying to harmonize with Josh as he strode the streets of his small home town. He raked a tall fence with a twig as he passed, adding a friendly percussion of hiss-TAK, hiss-TAK, hiss-TAK.

Josh rounded the corner of the fence and stopped dead in his tracks. Ahead of him stood the enemy. Several members of the school football team were clustered in front of McInery's liquor store drinking beers and laughing. Each one of them was wearing a blood red letter jacket, their names embroidered over their hearts.

It seemed that they hadn't spotted him yet, and Josh looked around frantically for an escape route. Before he could duck back around the fence, one of them shouted "Hey, Scrub!" Fear ran cold in Joshua's veins, and the sun was swallowed whole by dark, roiling clouds. "Get your ass over here."

He stood perfectly still, trembling like a rabbit, unable to move. The largest jock bellowed again. "I said, COME HERE you little prick!" Josh winced, spun on his heels and bolted.

"Where do you think you're going?" rang in his ears as he ran, panting for air. A half-empty bottle exploded as his feet, spraying his legs with beer and broken glass. Josh almost stumbled, but he somehow kept going.

He knew they were faster, he couldn't outrun them for long. He ducked into the open bay of an auto repair shop, cowering behind a rack of tires. He prayed that they didn't see where he went, or at least wouldn't follow him into a business where an adult might intervene.

From behind him, a gruff voice spat "what's the matter scrub?" Josh whipped around. In front of him stood a mechanic in a filthy blue jumpsuit, wiping the black grease from his hands. Somehow, the bright red jacket he was wearing over his work clothes was immaculate. He smiled sadistically. "You gonna cry, little baby?"

Reeling with panic, Josh darted out of the garage, running blindly down the street. He turned corners wildly, until he felt he had lost his pursuers. He slowed to a stop, supporting himself with his hands on his knees. He was breathing hard, a sharp pain in his side. When he had regained his breath, he slowly began shuffling down the street again.

Across the street stood a group of four girls he recognized from school but couldn't recall their names. They were all wearing letter jackets, pointing at Josh and laughing cruelly. Josh hurried on.

As he crossed Main St, the blast from a whistle startled Josh, and he turned to find a cop standing in the middle of the intersection, directing traffic. He too was wearing a red jacket over his uniform. The cop smiled evilly and flipped Josh off. Josh ran.

Spruce Street. "Almost home," Josh muttered thankfully as he turned the final corner. Ahead he could see the mailman making his appointed rounds, wearring in the same blood red jacket as everyone else. The Maxwells, Josh's next door neighbors, emerged onto their porch, clad in red and pointing at Josh, laughing as he sprinted up the walk to his front door. He threw the door open, flung himself inside, and slammed it closed behind him, slapping frantically at the deadbolt. Finally safe,

Josh mopped the sweat from his face with his sleeve and tried to regain his breath.

From the kitchen, Josh's mom shouted "Josh? Is that you?"

"Yeah mom, It's me," Josh panted.

"I'm making some deviled eggs. Are you hungry?"

Josh smiled. "Yeah, that would be great." Josh stepped out of the foyer and into the kitchen, but froze at the threshold. Inside the kitchen, both of his parents were wearing red letter jackets. On each breast cursive embroidery spelled out 'Mom" and 'Dad.' His mother was holding a tray full of deviled eggs, only instead of the traditional yellow filling was a sickly-looking runny red goo. Josh's father pinched one of the eggs from the tray and held it out towards Josh.

"Here's your egg, scrub!" He threw the egg at Josh's head but missed, the egg splattering against the doorframe, showering Josh with the blood-like yolk. Josh screamed and ran away, his parents' hysterical laughter echoing behind him.

He leaped into his room, slamming and locking the door behind him, then scrambled to push the dresser in front of the door, The maniacal laugher still rang in the hall beyond.

"Hey, Kid."

Josh whipped around terrified. The Man was standing there, silhouetted against the sunlight blazing in through the undulating curtains. As always, he was dressed all in black, his long cowboy-style duster flapping around his calves, his raven hair scattered haphazardly across his wrinkled face and across one eye like crosshairs.

His back pressed against the dresser, Josh whispered "get out of here."

"You can't run forever." He pulled a gleaming, chromed revolver out of his coat pocket, and twirled it around his finger like a movie cowboy.

"I... I can try," muttered Josh, wiping tears out of his eyes.

The Man smiled slightly. "No, you can't. I'm not done with you yet." He pointed the gun directly at Josh's face. Josh screamed and threw his arms up defensively as the gun erupted with a roar...

Josh Webster jolted upright in his bed, screaming at the top of his lungs, his gaunt face a rictus of terror, his deep-set eyes ringed with dark bags. In the darkness, his wife Claire added the harmony of a soprano shriek as she spastically scrambled out from under the covers. Light suddenly stabbed at Josh's eyes, and he flung his arms up against the glare.

"Jesus Christ, Josh, what the hell?"

Josh lowered his arms and squinted . Claire's face was as white as the sheet she had pulled from the bed and clutched against her chest, her hands trembling. She stood next to the light switch by the door of their bedroom, breathing hard.

Josh hung his head, exhausted and ashamed. "I'm okay."

"Well, I'm sure the hell *not* okay!"

"I'm sorry."

"Jesus Christ!! What time is it?"

Josh glanced at his bedside clock. "Almost three thirty."

Furious, Claire shook her head with disbelief. Without another word, she wadded up the bed sheet and threw it at Josh, then picked up her fuzzy pink robe from the floor and put it on. She stepped into a threadbare pair of slippers and shuffled out of the room. Josh watched her go, then began summoning the strength to get up himself.

He padded barefoot into the kitchen in his underwear, paused in the doorway, and leaned against the frame. Claire was pissed, slamming cupboard doors as she got down a bowl and began filling it with cereal.

"What are you doing? He asked softly."

"Having breakfast. What does it look like?"

"You don't have to be up for two hours."

"Well, that's too bad, because there's no way I'm going back to sleep now."

He stepped past her to retrieve a glass, then went back to the fridge and filled it halfway with orange juice and sat it down. Claire watched him pointedly as he opened the cupboard beneath the sink and produced a very large but mostly empty bottle of vodka. He emptied it into the orange juice, filling the glass right to the brim. He took a sip off the top of it without picking it up, then stirred it with a dirty spoon that was laying on the counter.

"Oh, that's just great." Clair spat.

"Breakfast of champions," Josh muttered, lifting the glass as if toasting her, and taking a deep swallow.

"Is that the bottle I bought two days ago?"

Josh shrugged noncommittally. Claire dropped her spoon into her cereal bowl and marched out of the room, glaring at Josh as she stomped past.

"Claire…"

She didn't slow down. Josh followed her back into the bedroom. Claire had the closet door open and was beginning to pull clothes out.

"Claire, look, I'm sorry…." He stammered.

She stopped and turned to stare at him. "Are you going to do this every morning from now on?

Josh grimaced. "I… I don't know. I haven't had the dreams for years."

"Well, how long did they last before?"

Josh took another swig from the glass and looked down. "Ten years."

Claire stood with her mouth open for a moment, then simply closed it, and returned to putting on her nurse's uniform.

"Look, it's not like I'm doing it on purpose…"

Claire shrugged. "I know that. But I have to be at work at six thirty sharp, and I have to hit the ground running. I can't keep waking up to the random adrenaline alarm clock every night."

"What do you want me to do about it?"

"I *told* you what I want you to do about it."

Josh shook his head. "You don't understand. I went through *years* of therapy as a kid. I saw every damned specialist on the West Coast, and a couple of 'em in New York. My parents spent a fortune on shrinks and none of them ever did anything that really helped.

She perched on the edge of the bed and began tying her clunky white shoes. "Yeah? Well you aren't a kid this time. You can't just drink yourself numb for fourteen years again.

"Why not? It worked before?"

"Clearly, it *didn't*. And besides, it would kill you. And that's assuming that I don't kill you first."

She stood up and walked away. Josh followed her into the bathroom where she began putting on her makeup. Josh stood in the doorway behind her, where she could see him in the mirror. "You look like hell."

"Thanks."

"I mean it."

"Maybe it's because I feel like shit."

"You need help," she said, making that funny face she always made as she put on her mascara. "Why won't you talk to someone?"

"I already told you. Because it's a waste of time."

Clair whipped around, one eyelash finished, looking like Alex from *A Clockwork Orange*. "No, what's a waste of time is living with you when you're like this. You're a mess, Josh. And you're turning me into a mess too." She opened her mouth like she was about to add something, then stopped, her face softening. She stepped closer and put her arms around him. "I love you, but it's killing me to see you in so much pain.

"I can deal with it. I've dealt with it for years."

She took his face gently in her hands and looked deeply into his eyes. "Well, I haven't. And I can't." She lightly stroked his hair out of his eyes, gave him a sad smile. After a moment of silence, Josh closed his eyes and nodded.

"Thank you," she said, and returned to the mirror. "I'll make an appointment for you."

Josh bristled slightly. "With who?"

"We've got several good psychiatrists on staff at the hospital. Unless there's someone else you'd rather go to.

He squirmed uncomfortably, but shook his head and retreated from the bathroom, defeated. From behind him, Clair said, gently, "Don't worry. It'll all be O.K."

In the hallway, Josh froze, his eyes wide with terror.

* * *

Josh slouched in an overstuffed chair in the waiting room. He was wearing his usual all-black uniform, 501 jeans, engineer boots, an obscure band t-shirt, and the motorcycle jacket he always wore like a carapace. In his mind, he looked like the old ad for Maxell cassette tapes, the one with a slick looking guy in aviator shades draped comfortably in a Corbusier chair facing a huge speaker, his tie flung backwards by the sheer power of the audio. Josh glanced up at the twenty-something receptionist and realized that not only had she probably never seen the ad, it was highly unlikely that she even knew what a cassette tape was. As he adjusted his internal perspective, he decided that she probably thought he looked homeless. He picked up a random magazine to hide behind and began flipping pages without looking at them.

The receptionist's phone rang, and she picked it up, nodded, and sat it back down. "Josh? She's ready for you."

Josh slowly climbed to his feet, and shuffled towards the door.

The woman who glanced up as he entered looked high-forties to mid fifties, short hair going grey at the sides, kind of attractive in a slightly severe, overly wholesome way. She smiled. "You must be Josh."

"Guilty as charged." Josh muttered with resignation, flopping down into the chair facing her desk. He slouched as if he were trying to pull his head into his coat like a turtle..

I'm Dr. Mendel. You can call me Sylvia if you prefer."

Josh nodded, looking around the office.

"Claire told me that you were reluctant to come. Thanks for giving me a chance."

Josh shrugged. "What chance? You get paid whether you make me better or not."

"Am I supposed to make you better?"

She shook her head. "Not really. I guide people towards helping themselves. Since you are here, I have to assume that there's something in your life that you want to change. If that's not correct, we're just wasting each other's time. If you want to go, there's no fee for today."

Josh stared at her, sizing her up. She was still smiling, but her face had taken on some delicate edge.

"Look, I've been to a lot of shrinks over the years. Most of them have looked at me like I was a car that wasn't running right. They put me up on blocks, ran some tests, poked me and prodded me, gave me some drugs and then told me I was depressed. Like I didn't already know that."

Dr. Mendel nodded. "I promise that I won't do that to you."

He stared a bit longer. "OK, where do you want to start?"

"Where do *you* want to start?"

He took a deep breath, resigning himself to the process. "I want to start by getting rid of these fucking nightmares."

She leaned back in her chair. "OK, how long have you been having them?"

"Since I was fifteen years old. I grew up in a suburb of Los Angeles, just a little too near the inner city to be really safe, but far enough away to preserve the illusion. My parents were content with that balance, but then, they weren't fifteen."

* * *

School was a cross between a juvenile detention center and a zoo, only the animals weren't kept in their cages, and were kicked out of the compound at 3:00, let loose on the world at large.

The bell meant freedom and terror, pressure and chaos. The school doors would slam open like countless mouths and vomit out streams of screaming kids in all directions. The halls were torrents of motion and compression, surging outward in whatever direction put up the least resistance. The small were pushed to the sides, and with faces grinding against the locker-lined walls, acting as sort of a human lubricant to glide the masses outward. I was small, so I spent a lot of time getting to know the lockers.

Worse still, if you were swept into a space between banks of lockers, you stayed there unless you could force your way back into the stream, but if you were strong enough to do that, you didn't get lodged in the first place.

Sometimes smart can make up for strong. I would use leverage and velocity to my advantage, rolling my body this way and that, not entirely unlike body surfing, to stay as near the middle as I could, so I rarely got stuck.

That day, I was *placed*.

I can still feel the steel grip of huge club-like hands on my shoulders. Strength that at the time seemed super-human lifted me of my feet, rotated me through the crowd which parted and splashed like water, and planted me firmly with my face against the wall in the pressureless vortex between lockers. Then the hands were gone.

I spun about furious and terrified, but my tormentor was gone, swept along down the human rapids. I heard a beefy laugh, and caught the flash of an eye glancing back over a red-jacket shoulder; one of the sub-human football thugs that were the bane of my existence. To play football at my school one had to be an utterly brain-dead sadistic moose in eternal mating frenzy. Those were the *nice* ones.

I fumed, near the point of tears, looking at the blur of bodies rushing past me, despairing. If there was just one person smaller than me, I could shove my way back into the flow in front of them without getting my teeth shattered. Most anyone smaller than me hung out in the chess club until the melee was over. I didn't have that option because I had a bus to catch.

After what seemed like life in prison, the raw human density dropped enough that I was able to push back out into the hall. I was shoved roughly from behind for having the nerve to put myself between someone and the door, and went sprawling across the freshly waxed floor. At least I was nimble, and was able to scramble back to my feet before getting trampled.

Of course, once outside the threshold of the door, the entire mass of previously hysteric cattle came to a complete stop to don shades, exchange plans or phone numbers, or just loiter and look cool. The resulting log jam was yet another gauntlet to run, and the my random path through the crowd, shaped by jostles and shoves, finally released me at the wrong end of the school. I hit the crowded sidewalk running, dodging assailants as I sprinted toward the bus stop. I arrived in time to see the yellow smoking brick that was my ticket home receding into the distance.

Normally, I would've said that the bus was invented as a method to interrogate foreign agents in South America. That would be if I'd made it. I longed for that bus like a departing lover as I watched it disappear. Home was nearly two miles away.

I'd walked home before, but was already on the verge of crying, wanting to scream with rage and frustration, and exhausted from the tension of just another day in hell. I slung my bookbag and started away from the din.

Slowly, I began to relax. The howling oppression of the school faded behind me as I got deeper into suburbia. Soon, all I could hear was the quiet rhythm of my footsteps punctuated by the zip zip of my nylon bookbag brushing against my corduroy pants, and the occasional songbird. It was a nice day, with spring drawing near, so I took off my coat and tied it around my waist. Walking home wasn't going to be so bad after all.

Then I saw a flash of red.

They came around the corner ahead of me, four of them, clutching beer bottles. They were chuckling obliviously to each other, walking that swaggering walk that looked like something was stuck up their asses. I froze in dread as their slow motion gazes swung around and locked onto me, stupid, evil smiles crystallizing on their predatory faces.

"Well well well. Look who we have here!" one of them smarmed, while another tongued the inside of his cheek like he was trying to dislodge some extraordinarily nasty idea from between his teeth. I started to turn around to look for an escape route, only to find three more red letter jackets coming down the sidewalk behind me.

"Hey Chuck!" boomed one of the first group. "Look what we found!"

There simply were no words for the sickening sense of loss and agony I felt. I wanted to throw up, I prayed vehemently to God to *make them go away oh please just let this be a nightmare let me wake up I'll do anything...* and knowing full well that it was real, it was happening, that there was no escape this time.

"Isn't this the little fucker who narked on Willie?"

Now I was doomed. I hadn't narked on anyone; no one was stupid enough to say anything about what went on at that school despite the number of felonies witnessed on a daily basis, not even the faculty. Nonetheless, Willie had been arrested, the police came in force, pried his locker open with a crowbar while they held him there in handcuffs screaming and writhing, and carried him and a large bag full of white powder out to the car and off to jail.

Not that this had anything to do with me, it was merely the excuse. These thick-skulled Neanderthals didn't even have the decency to pound someone without the pretense of some fictitious reason, so they made one up on the spot, you said shit about so-in-so, you took something from my locker, *you narked on Willie.*

Only this time, the reason came charged with so much inherent anger that I could see in their eyes — like those of a snarling dog — that I was going to get the treatment that they would given the actual snitch.

I started yammering automatically; "It wasn't me, I wouldn't nark on anybody, I never say anything I..." but I knew there could be no reasoning with these assholes. First came the shove to the chest that was invariably their opening, hard enough to shatter rock. I hit the ground hard like I hadn't passed through the intervening space, my head bouncing off the sidewalk, ringing like a bell. Fire erupted behind my eyes and surged through my entire body.

Suddenly, One of them yanked from the ground by the front of my shirt and slammed against a fence. My vision was swimming with tears and disorientation, but I could see that they had formed a half circle around me and the one holding me, glancing over their shoulders for cops and acting as a curtain against witnesses.

Completely missing was the usual stream of verbal abuse, the "Hey faggot, here's what we do to snitches" bullshit .They weren't saying *anything*. I realized that this was even more serious than I thought. Then I saw the knife.

One of the blockers brought it out of his jacket pocket, handing it over almost ritually to Chuck, the quarterback and therefore their leader, who took it without looking away from me or letting go of my shirt. He held it up in front of my face and pressed the button. The blade flashed out like a striking cobra, elegantly deadly.

I flinched as he brought the point to my forehead, pulling my face away. With lightning speed he grabbed my hair and yanked my face around to stare at the knife. I closed my eyes as he traced the bridge of my nose with the point, and down to my mouth.

Opening my eyes, I felt a line of sharp line of itching pain down my nose. He had scratched me slightly, just enough to burn with the salty sweat pouring down my trembling face. He smiled with one side of his face, looking away from me for the first time since he'd grabbed me. He grinned for a moment at his buddies, as if looking for a sign, or just making sure everyone was looking. Some returned his grin, others looked merely hypnotized by the intensity of the moment. Then he turned back to me and the smile was gone.

Oh God, here it comes... echoed through my mind as if someone else had said it and he brought his arm back. I wish I had closed my eyes but somehow, some primal part of me couldn't look away. He began the plunge toward my clenched stomach when his head came apart.

Like an overripe watermelon, the insides of his head broke through his shattering skull and were strewn all over the still smiling goons surrounding me. The smiles melted as the sound of thunder slapped them into awareness that they were showered in blood, brains and bone shrapnel. His body heaved wildly, throwing the knife skillessly towards the ground where it clattered to a stop against my sneakers, followed momentarily by his lifeless bulky frame.

The others scattered like pigeons, except for one: Johnny, who'd been Chuck's closest friend and constant companion. He stared in shock at the body on the ground, his red jacket hiding the blood it was soaked with, unlike his gore-covered face. He slowly brought his gaze up to focus down the street to see where the shot had come from, then was flung back abruptly as the top of his head was torn away and scattered. He slapped the sidewalk on his back and never moved again.

I forced myself to look. *He* was standing about ten yards away, legs spread, still holding the gun out like in some police movie. He was dressed in black from head to toe, and draped in a black coat so long that it nearly touched the ground. He stood frozen for a long time, still staring at where Johnny had stood. Then, very slowly, he lowered the gun, and looked at me.

He looked as scared as I was, trembling visibly even at that distance. The gun dangled limply at his side for a moment, then he dropped it, and it clattered to the sidewalk. He staggered a little, clutching his stomach, and I began to wonder if he hadn't been shot too. He stumbled over to the bushes against the fence and threw up.

After a while, he quit puking, wiped his mouth on his coat and still leaning against the fence, turned back to face me.

"You, you O.K. kid?"

I was huddled on the ground against the fence, shaking so hard my teeth were chattering, tears and snot gushing down my face. I was dizzy with the shock and the adrenaline that seemed to have replaced all my blood and the searing line down my nose. "Y-y-y-yeah" I squeaked feebly.

Slowly, he took his weight off of the fence and stood up, and shuffled slowly toward me. I skittered back away from him like a crab, and he stopped, holding his hands out. "I'm not going to hurt you. It's O.K. now. It's O.K." He spoke soothingly, but stared at me intensely, like there was something wrong with me. He crouched down where he was. "I won't come any closer".

Out of the corner of my eye I could see the bodies and the spreading puddles of blood, but steered my gaze away.

"Listen kid." He kept staring at me, crazed, terrified. "Listen. I, I can't stay." He laughed humorlessly, a single raspy bark that made me jump. "I've got to go now. You'll be fine. But listen. This is very important. You will see me again." I was shaking my head almost imperceptibly no, but he held his hand up. "Don't worry, I won't hurt you, I promise. I swear."

He heard it before I did, and looked up, listening. Then it reached me as well. The sharp whine of distant sirens, growing louder.

"I'm sorry, kid. I, ah..." he seemed to be wrestling with his own mind, than spat "oh shit." and backed down the sidewalk to where he'd dropped the gun. He stooped to pick it up, but never took his eyes from mine.

"Go ahead and tell them everything. It's O.K. Don't worry, it'll all be O.K." Then, with what seemed a great summoning of will, he turned away and ran off around the corner.

* * *

Dr. Mendel was sitting bolt upright in her chair like an old-fashioned school marm, her eyes soft with sympathy and compassion. Josh slumped in his chair, his eyes focused on something very far away.

"When the police got there they bundled me up in an army surplus blanket they pulled from the trunk. It smelled like something dead. Then they put me in the back seat of the car. I sat there for a long time, while they took pictures. One of them asked me what happened. I wasn't able to talk to them for a long time.

"Eventually they took me to the station, and I was able to give them my phone number. My folks came down to pick me up, my mom was crying, my dad just looked uncomfortable. I told them what happened, and they got it down on tape so they could transcribe it. I still have a copy of the transcription, but I never read it. I don't need to."

Josh looked up, seeing what looked like genuine hurt in Dr. Mendel's eyes. He grinned broadly, he'd seen this before. "Pretty fucked up, eh?

She nodded. "It's horrible." She dabbed at the corner of her eye with a tissue, quickly reassembling her professional composure. "Did the dreams start immediately?"

Josh laughed bitterly. "Oh yeah, that very first night. At first they were just replays of what actually happened. But over time, they started to *change*. In one of the early ones, Chuck – that's the jock who was gonna stab me – he's crucified on the fence with a switchblade knife stuck through the center of each hand. The ground is littered with scores of bodies, all dead football players. The Man comes up to me and puts the gun in my hands. It is cold and very heavy. 'You do it this time' he says. I pull the gun up and hold like I've seen in movies, like he did, and slowly take aim at Chuck's forehead.

"Chuck is crying. He says 'I didn't mean anything by it, it was a joke, I promise I'll never give you a hard time ever again...'

"It's as far as he gets when I pull the trigger and his head explodes in slow motion spraying red pulp and watermelon seeds all over the fence, the slat behind his head breaking off and spinning away, leaving the fence looking like Alfred E. Newman's grin. After that, The Man just looks at me, nodding and smiling.

"And the worst part is, if feels damned good."

Dr. Mendel nodded. "That's understandable. After the persecution and the trauma, feelings of retribution are…"

"Are perfectly natural," Josh interrupted. "Sure. I've heard it a million times. But you know what? It does exactly *squat* to make me feel better. It makes me sick to know that such hatred, such violence is stored up inside me."

She looked at Josh, quizzically. "That's a strong reaction. That dream didn't sound all that severe."

Josh barked a mirthless laugh. "You're right, that was nothing. That was one of the *good* dreams. Try this one on for size…

"I walk into the school. The Man is standing just inside the doorway, and he passes me the gun real discretely so no one sees, and I pocket it. I cruise the halls, ignoring all those around me. Then I see a red jacket. It's Willie, rummaging through the bags of cocaine in his locker, tons of them. I pull the gun out, take aim, and blow him all over the lockers. The shot echoes through the halls and comes back to me about eight times. Emotionlessly, I pull his letter jacket off the way one would skin a chicken before frying it, and put it on.

"I continue down the hall. Chuck rounds a corner and his eyes light up with recognition, because somehow, with his jacket on, I look just like Willie. Chuck is reaching out to shake hands when I pull the gun out and shoot him dead between his eyes. He slides across the freshly waxed floor into the space between banks of lockers and stops with his head against the wall at a strange angle. I pull his jacket off and put it on over the one I'm already wearing. It fits perfectly.

"I come to a set of swinging double doors night as well have "HELL" engraved on them. They open into the boy's locker room, a warren of pungent lockers and showers. *Their turf.* I walk through those doors like they lead into an old-time western saloon.

"They're all in there, every last member of the football team. One by one, I blow their asses all over the room. One by one I take their coats and I put them on. Soon the entire room is knee-deep with corpses and blood, and the only one left is Johnny.

"I guess this is yours." he says, defeated, and he takes off his jacket, holding it out to me. I look back over my shoulder. The Man is there, smiling and nodding. "It'll all be O.K." he says, and I turn back to Johnny and I *waste him.*"

Josh stopped and leaned forward, checking Dr. Mendel for a reaction, but she was poker-faced. "Is 'The Man' always in your dreams?"

Josh nodded solemnly. "Always."

"Does he ever tell you his name?"

"Nope, he doesn't need to. He's *The Man.* There isn't another."

Josh squirmed in his seat as she paused, jotting some notes in her pad.

"Look, Dr. Mendel, can I make this easy for you? I know this drill by heart." She gestured for him to continue. "I am dealing with textbook post-traumatic stress disorder. I had one shrink who specialized in Vietnam vets, helping them deal with what they experienced in combat. He said I was as bad as any of them."

She raised her eyebrows, but Josh couldn't tell if it was in shock or disapproval. "He said that to you?"

"Well, not in those words, but when you cut through the polite bullshit, that was the gist of it."

"OK, since we're being so clinical, what are the rest of your symptoms?"

"The whole nine yards. Ballistophobia, paranoia, alienation, disorientation, flashback, clinical depression."

"Substance abuse?"

Josh smiled. "Yeah, you could say that. Alcohol and downers mostly. Psychedelics were out of the question. Made that ugly mistake once and *only* once. I really just wanted to be numb."

"For how long?"

"Better part of ten years. Until it was over."

"The dreams stopped?"

Josh nodded. "*Everything* stopped. I quit worrying about who was following me. I could go outside in broad daylight without constantly looking for escape routes. I quit recoiling from every loud sound.

"I knew the worst was over the fourth of July when I was twenty-five, when I didn't spend it with earplugs in and a pillow wrapped around my head, and actually went outside onto the front porch, and looked up at the fireworks blossoming in the sky. Man, those sparkling colored lights were beautiful, and I knew how they felt. That year, the fireworks were just for me.

"That was twelve years ago. It's almost funny how the Fourth took on new meaning to me, that every year I could stand tall in the face of the sharp report of gunpowder explosions without quailing would fill me with a fierce pride that had absolutely nothing to do with God And Country or patriotism and everything to do with Independence."

Dr. Mendel was smiling. Josh matched her. "Pretty fucking dramatic, eh?"

Her smile grew. "It is!! You had a breakthrough!! That's fantastic!"

"Yeah?" Josh's smile melted into a scowl. "Well it's all shot to shit now."

* * *

Josh sighed as he turned the key in his front door and made his way into the apartment. He wriggled out of his jacket and threw it over the chair.

From the kitchen, Claire shouted "Josh? Is that you?"

"Yup." Josh muttered, shuffling into the kitchen where Claire was making dinner. He kissed her on the back of the head as she chopped vegetables."

"How did it go?"

"Perfect. She's says I'm cured and I don't ever have to go back."

Josh produced a pint of vodka from the paper sack he was carrying and began to pour a drink.

Claire stopped chopping and turned to glare at him. Josh shrugged. "It was pretty much your standard first visit. She sat there and listened attentively while I treated her to The Josh Webster Show."

Clair sighed and returned to the chopping. "Did you ever think that the reason therapy never helped you was that you didn't take it seriously?"

He sipped his screwdriver and nodded. "It's hard to take it seriously after a while. After the umpteenth shrink you start recognizing key phrases, like they all read it out of the same books."

"That's because they do. But it doesn't change the fact that you are only going to get out of it what you put into it. If you go in with a chip on your shoulder, *daring* them to make you well, it ain't gonna happen."

Josh shrugged. "Yeah, I know. It just feels like I should be able to work through this by myself."

"Why? Because you are so tough? Because you're a man? What makes you so different from anybody else? Josh shrugged, and Claire turned to look him in the eye. "We all need help every now and then. There's nothing wrong with accepting it, or even making it happen. Josh nodded sheepishly. "So, when is your next appointment?"

Josh looked at his feet and mumbled. "I didn't make one."

Claire looked up, her eyes filled with anger and disappointment.

"I told her I wanted to think it over."

After a moment, Claire scowled, and then returned to her chopping. "Don't think it over too long."

* * *

Thirty-seven year old Joshua Webster sat uncomfortably in the cramped seat of a school bus. He looked forlornly out the window at the passing hometown scenery of his childhood. He looked around at the perfectly normal kids sitting around him, they stole occasional glances at him, sizing him up.

Even from behind, there was no mistaking the driver. It was The Man, and he was staring pointedly at Josh in the rear view mirror.

Looking around again, Josh noticed that the kids were all giggling at him, like they were all in on some secret joke. Josh slid out of his seat and walked slowly down the aisle towards the front of the bus, bracing himself against the bumpy motion of the bus on the seat backs. He stopped just behind The Man.

"So, where are we going?"

"It's a school bus. Where do you think we're going?"

Josh shook his head. "I don't go there anymore."

The Man looked up from the road. "You can't skip class. You'll flunk."

"But I already graduated."

A wad of paper hit Josh in the back of the head. He whipped around, annoyed, looking for whoever threw it. All the kids made the pantomime of avoiding his gaze, innocently.

"Well then, I guess you must be the driver."

Confused, Josh turned back to The Man, only he wasn't there. The driver's seat was empty, and the bus was careening wildly into oncoming traffic. The kids began screaming as Josh leapt into the seat, grabbing the wheel and tried to gain control, but it was too late. The bus crashed headlong into a gasoline truck, and the world erupted into fire...

Dr. Mendel sat silently for a moment. Josh's whole body was a knot of tension, his hands trembling slightly. "This one hit you pretty hard."

He nodded emphatically. "Yeah, and I'm not sure why. It's certainly no worse than any of the other dreams I've had, but man, it's really fucked me up."

"And you've never had this specific dream before? Nothing even similar?

He shook his head. "No, they've all been new lately."

"And that scares you?"

"Damn straight it scares me! It's all starting again! On the drive here I thought someone was following me!"

"Were they?"

"Of course not. They turned off two exits before me. Doesn't mean I didn't keep watching for them."

She nodded. "Have you been doing the breathing exercises I showed you?"

"Yes."

"Are they helping?"

"No."

Dr. Mendel took off her glasses and rubbed her eyes in frustration.

"Fed up with me yet?" Josh grinned.

"No, Josh, I just don't think you're trying very hard."

"I'm doing everything you said to do." He grabbed his backpack from where it leaned against the side of his chair and dug a book out of it. "I've read the book on dream analysis." He set the book on her desk and produced another. "I've read the book on lucid dreaming." He set it down on top of the first book, and pulled a tattered looking notebook from the pack. "I've been keeping a

journal and writing down every dream I have in intimate detail."
He slapped the notebook on top of the stack.

"You have?"

Josh dropped the limp backpack beside the chair, slumped back
into his seat, and nodded uncomfortably.

Dr. Mendel picked up the notebook delicately. "May I look at it?"

Josh shrugged noncommittally. She opened the notebook and began
thumbing through the pages, which were crammed with a lot of
writing, small and intricate, and punctuated with the occasional
crude sketch.

"Josh, this is amazing!" Josh shrugged again. "I mean it! Have you
been going back and reading them?"

"Yeah. Every night before bed."

She continued scanning the notebook, delighted and spellbound.
"And have you been noticing any patterns?"

Josh didn't answer. After a moment, Dr. Mendel stopped and looked
up at him over the tops of her glasses. "Josh?"

Josh squirmed uncomfortably, clearly not wanting to talk about it.
After a moment, he nodded.

"Yeah. There's a running theme."

Pleased, she said, "That's great! What did you find?"

"Well, lately they've all involved me as an adult, rather than as a
kid.

"What else?"

"In most of them, one way or another…"

"Yes?"

"I go *back*." His gaze turned inward.

"Go back where?"

Josh gritted his teeth. "To where it happened."

Dr. Mendel paused, sizing up Josh's discomfort, gauging how hard she should probe. "What do you think it means?"

"I don't know."

"Not even a guess?"

Josh wrapped his arms around himself. "I think… I think that *something* wants me to go back. Or, maybe, thinks that I *should*."

She nodded. "Don't forget that everything you see and hear in dreams is an extension of *you*."

He scowled. "Fine. Then some part of *me* wants to go back."

She sat back in her chair, quietly pleased. "And how does that make you feel?"

Josh looked up, suddenly very focused and angry. "How do you think it makes me feel?" he spat. "It scares the shit out of me! I haven't been back there since the day it happened. My parents put me in a different school so that I wouldn't have to face that place ever again. I left home when I started college, and I've never even been back to visit my parents in their own home since." He pressed his lips into a tight line.

"What is it that you are hiding from?"

"What do you mean?"

"Do you think there's still something there that can hurt you?

He shrugged. "I don't know. Probably not."

"Then why does the thought of going back scare you so much?"

Josh looked away. "I just don't want to have to relive it."

She smiled gently at him. "Aren't you reliving it every night anyway?"

He started to respond, but had no answer.

* * *

Josh flopped an overnight bag on the bed, unzipped it and flung it open. It smelled vaguely stale and musty from years of disuse.

"How long has it been?" Claire asked, standing in her nightgown and brushing her teeth.

"Twelve years."

"It's funny. In all the time we've been together, I've never seen where you grew up."

He shrugged. "You're not missing much."

"You've been to *my* parent's house."

"*Your* parents live across town."

He opened the closet. Josh's wardrobe was comically monochromatic, an inky pit of darkness. He pulled out a couple of pairs of jeans and threw them unceremoniously into the bag. Claire had vanished back into the bathroom to spit. Josh continued tossing clothes in the bag until he looked at it dissatisfied, but zipped it closed anyway.

Claire re-emerged, ready for bed. She wrapped her arms around Josh and pulled him down to the edge of the bed and kissed him softly. "I'm going to miss you."

"Not as much as I'm going to miss you."

"How long do you think you'll be gone?"

He shrugged. "I dunno. A couple of days."

She held him close, nestling her head in his shoulder. He wrapped his arms around her, but continued staring into the distance.

"Are you scared?"

He sighed. "Yeah, a little. But I honestly don't know why."

She ran her fingers through his hair. "Isn't that why you're going?"

* * *

Josh walked down the jetway towards the terminal at LAX, his bag slung from a strap over his shoulder. Through the kaleidoscope of fellow travelers, he spotted his parents where they waited, hiding their trepidation under a mask of happiness and excitement. Josh pushed his way through the crowd and hugged them both.

"Hello, Son."

"Hey Pop. Hi Mom."

Mrs. Webster stood back a pace. "You look great! Have you lost a little weight?"

"Yeah, I've been hitting the gym again."

Mr. Webster patted him on the shoulder. "Good for you. That always did seem to help a bit."

The mood ground to an awkward halt with the first reminder of why Josh was back. Mrs. Webster scrambled for a save. "Do you have any bags to pick up?"

Josh shook the bag with his shoulder. "Nope, this is it." He could read something like a vague disappointment in his mother's eyes, but the look in his father's was unmistakably *relief*.

Mr. Webster smiled as they began down the concourse. "It's nice having you come visit us for a change."

Josh smiled wryly. "I'm sure."

"You hungry?" asked Mrs. Webster. "We could stop somewhere and grab some breakfast."

"Not really."

Josh sat quietly for most of the drive back, engaging in polite small talk just enough that his parents could keep nattering to keep the silence at bay. He gazed out the window as they glided down the off ramp and onto the streets of his old hometown.

His father glanced up in the rear view mirror. "The old town's changed a lot since the last time you were here."

Josh shrugged. "Not that much."

His mother turned around in her seat to face him. "They finally tore down the old car wash. There's a strip mall there now."

"Can't get enough strip malls." Josh muttered sarcastically.

His mom either didn't notice or pretended not to. "It's very nice. We even have a McDonalds now! Can you believe it? We're practically a real town!"

Josh smiled distantly, watching as they progressed down familiar pathways to the place he once called home. The old neighborhood looked much the same for the most part, a few neighbors had repainted, one added a second floor, but there was no mistaking where he was. They pulled into the driveway, and Josh had to keep reminding himself that this time it wasn't a dream as they walked up to the front door.

With a jangling of keys, Mr. Webster opened the door and lead the way in. Josh followed close behind, and found himself in a completely unfamiliar place. The lines were mostly the same, but a wall had been taken out between the dining room and the kitchen, the furniture and wall coverings were all new. He wrestled with the dissonance between this place, and the place he had visited so many times in his sleep.

"Wow, you remodeled."

Mrs. Webster smiled uneasily. "Oh, we did this years ago. Do you like it?"

He looked around as if lost. "I guess it just never occurred to me that it would be any different.

Mr. Webster said "Everybody changes, son. Even your parents."

Josh nodded. "Yeah, I guess so. Hey, where can I dump my bag?"

Mrs. Webster gestured down the hall. "In your old room. We've cleared it out for you!"

With a mix of curiosity and trepidation, Josh stepped down the hallway, and through the open door to the place that had once served as a sanctuary and a womb. But like the rest of the house, that place no longer existed. Feminine lacy curtains and floral wallpaper defined a space that had absolutely nothing to do with him. He put his bag down gently on a stranger's frilly bed, heaped with flouncy pillows.

"Wow, when you guys redo a place, you leave no stone unturned."

"We've mostly been using it for storage," his mother said nervously. "But when you called I asked your father to move the boxes out into the garage."

"Thanks," Josh said, still mesmerized. "Did you keep any of my stuff?"

Mr. Webster cleared his throat. "Of course. There's a couple of boxes up the attic if you want them."

Josh's eyes fell upon a framed photo standing on the dresser. It was a black and white portrait of the whole family, but Josh was about eight in the picture, happy and well adjusted. It was a picture of the time before everyone's life unraveled. Josh turned back to his father. "No. Feel free to chuck it all if you need the space."

* * *

Josh was awaken by sunlight streaming through the unfamiliar curtains, warming his face. He rolled over onto his back, stretching and blinking, and wrestling with complete disorientation, unable to glean where he was in either time or space.

He struggled into the same jeans he'd worn on the plane, feeling oddly rested and relaxed. He padded shirtless and shoeless into the still house.

"Mom? Dad?" he shouted, but got no reply. He wandered into the kitchen. Unlike most of the house, the kitchen still felt familiar. The appliances were new, and the countertops had been redone, but the space was still shaped by ritual and routines that had not changed in many years.

He instinctively knew where the cereal would be, right down to the brand. The bowls were still within easy reach of the same spot, the silverware drawer directly in front of him. The motions were so familiar it was like watching a favorite old movie. He sat the bowl on the table and went to the fridge for some milk. A note waited for him exactly where his mom knew to put it so that he would find it. He removed the ancient, familiar magnet shaped like an apple and read the note;

Dear Josh,

Your father is at work and I have to go help the ladies from the church with their canning. We'll both be back in time for dinner. Help yourself to anything in the kitchen and make yourself at home.

Love, Mom.

Josh sat the note down on the table, ate his cereal, and washed the bowl and spoon, leaving them in the dish drainer. He wondered why he didn't do that at home instead of just leaving the bowl in the sink for whoever got stuck with doing the piled up dishes. He felt sure that Claire would prefer it that way.

He found his way to the bathroom and started the shower. Here was the most unfamiliar room of all, his folks had clearly splurged when they redid the shower and sink with marble, it was like being at a fairly nice hotel. He sat a thick, plush towel aside and stepped under the stream of hot water. An old song sprang into his head as he washed, one that he hated as a kid because it had been big hit and got way too much play on the radio. In retrospect, he decided that it wasn't really a bad song, and he found himself humming the melody while he rinsed off. He returned to his room with a huge towel wrapped around his waist, drying his spiky hair with another.

Suddenly, a loud sound shattered the stillness, a loud *whump* against the side of the house. Adrenaline surged through Josh's veins, and he searched the room in a wild panic for the source of the noise. He had dropped his towels and was crouched, his hands out in front of him to ward off an unseen attacker. His heartbeat pounded like thunder in his ears, and the comfortable room constricted into a confining cell without enough air.

He rushed to the window to find the assailant, but the only thing he could see was a kid on bike riding leisurely away. The kid pulled a rolled up newspaper from the bag slung over his shoulders, and he sailed like a boomarang towards the next door neighbors' front door, where it hit the wall with a resounding *thwack*.

He laughed, a high pitched keening bordering on hysterical. He was still hyperventilating, and he leaned back against the wall and tried to get control of his breathing.

"Josh, are you OK?" his dad shouted from the doorway. Only it wasn't this doorway, it was the old doorway, his doorway. Josh cowered crying against his closet door, his floor sparkling with broken glass. Josh's mom crowded in behind his dad, both of them younger, strain apparent in their faces. "Are you hurt, Josh?"

Josh shook his head, but was very afraid.

"God damn it. That's the third time," his father shouted gruffly.

"Why can't they leave us alone?" his mother pleaded, near tears.

"Because they're good for nothing bastards, that's why. And I'm not gonna take it any more. If they want to mess with us again, I'm gonna put 'em down like mongrel dogs, I don't care how old they are."

Mrs. Webster helped Josh to his feet, brushing flecks of broken glass off of him with her apron. "We already talked about this. I don't want a gun in the house, not after what happened..."

"Christ, Helen," Mr. Webster spat angrily, "they won't touch him at school 'cause they're worried that psychopath might still be hanging around. I think it's time we give them a reason to leave him alone here as well."

Josh stood in the sunlight, in the unfamiliar room, watching the paperboy ride casually away. He looked around at the perfect room trying so hard to pretend it wasn't his room, but paint and wallpaper can only cover so much.

Going through the door to his parents' bedroom still felt *wrong*. He'd never been allowed in there as a kid, that was *their* sanctuary, the one place they could get away from the life that revolved around Joshua like he was its axle. Even empty, you could feel the vacuum, the absence of *him*. He walked purposefully towards his father's side of the bed, braced against the fear of being caught where he shouldn't be.

In the drawer next to the bed was his father's gun. It was a fairly old .38 police revolver, lying as if sleeping next to a box of ammunition. Josh picked it up and held it, looking at it for a long time. It felt too light, too small and delicate. It was the first time he had ever touched a real gun, which struck him as hilarious considering how many people he'd killed in his dreams.

He thumbed the release for the cylinder and flipped it opened with a casual gesture. He laughed that he knew how to do that merely from watching so many procedurals on T.V., and briefly wondered what that said about our society. One by one he slid bullets into the chambers, then snapped the cylinder back into place and tucked the gun in his jacket pocket.

As Josh stepped out onto the front porch, he paused a moment, wondering if the key he had been carrying all along would still work to lock the door. To his surprise, it did.

He walked, because it seemed the only way he had ever done it. He barely noticed the streets he'd trod so often in the past as he covered one square in the sidewalk after another. Things got less familiar as he got closer to downtown, businesses changed more frequently than residences. He felt himself tensing up automatically as he approached McInery's liquors, which had once been the favorite watering hole of the football zombies. Old man McInery had been a nice man, an honest man, but he'd been as scared of them as anyone. Now, McInery was long dead, and the store had become a "KwikStop", with neon and splashy graphics, a "convenience store" rather than the neighborhood liquor store. Two gaudily painted "monster trucks" were parked in front. Josh walked past quickly choking back an urge to cross the street, driven by old instincts that this was a dangerous place.

Josh felt bile rising at the back of his throat as he drew ever closer to the school. Having crossed the main drag, he was back in a residential area, and the old houses were remarkably unchanged. Even the birdsong seemed eerily familiar, as though it was bleeding through from another time.

With the tension becoming nearly audible, he rounded the last corner before he arrived, and stopped dead in his tracks the moment he could see down the street.

Ahead of him was a clump of red jackets, clustered around another smaller, younger kid. The backs of the jackets displayed the familiar gold "G", for Gryphons, the school mascot. The jackets hadn't changed much in twenty years, but then schools try to hang on to tradition where things like sports are concerned.

Then he saw the knife.

The one holding the kid against the fence pulled it out of his pocket, and flicked it open effortlessly. The six others were shielding the scene, but they couldn't hide it from Josh, because he knew it from the inside. Slowly, reflexively, he drew the gun.

They didn't seem to see him, completely mesmerized by what they were doing. They were all still small potatoes, and didn't get to see a murder every day. They weren't sure whether they liked it — no, a couple of them clearly did — but they knew that it was *important*.

The leader drew a line of scarlet down the bridge of the little kid's nose, and Josh's own nose burned in recognition. Fury swelled within him, an uncontrollable anger, and he drew a bead on the temple of the asshole with the knife.

The jock pulled his hand back for the stab, *Oh God, here it comes* echoed through Josh's head like someone else had said it and he pulled the trigger. The gun tried to fly away, but he managed to hold on to it. When he regained his footing, the one with the knife was lying on the ground in a puddle of crimson. The others put years of football practice into running away.

All but one, and Josh pointed the gun at his forehead.

He wanted to pull the trigger. He *needed* to pull the trigger. This lowlife was, for that moment, the apex of all he hated, the very embodiment of all that had caused him so many years of agony and suffering. Everything that had ever hurt him was suddenly congealed into one festering lump of vermin that was that boy...

...who stood there, staring at Josh, showing nothing on his face but hurt and shock and the loss his best friend.

"Run, you idiot," Josh rasped.

The kid just stood there, working his mouth soundlessly, tears streaming down his face. Josh knew that he couldn't hold back his rage much longer.

"RUN!" he screamed.

Something in the boy gave, and he ran.

Something in Josh gave, and everything span and the raisin bran he had for breakfast sprayed up his nose and all over the Juniper bushes. He kept puking until his stomach was empty and then he puked some more. Eventually he was able to stand up, and he turned to see the kid collapsed against the fence, shaking like an out-of-balance washing machine. Josh's eyes were torn to the little box clipped on the kid's belt. *An iPod, fer Christ's sake, I never had a fucking iPod...*

The kid looked a lot like Josh did at that age, but not *quite* enough, and the clothes were all wrong...

"Hey, kid, uh, you alright?" Josh winced because he clearly wasn't and everything was echoing funny like they were in a gymnasium.

"Y-y-y-eah" the kid slurred. He looked as though he was trying to push back through the fence to the other side. There was a fine line of red down the center of his face from just between his eyebrows to the tip of his nose.

"I'm Sorry," Josh stammered, "really."

"O-k-k-k-kay" the kid stuttered.

Josh fought for orientation, trying hard not to black out. "You'll be fine." He muttered. "Trust me." He wanted to slap himself for his inadequacy. "Look, just tell them everything. I wish I could tell you more but, but, you'll see me again." Josh wished it didn't sound so much like a threat. The kid looked away, and he knew he was blowing it.

The faint whine of sirens shrieked in the distance. Josh whispered, "I've got to go."

The kid nodded, hiding his face, pink tears dripping off the end of his nose.

He started to leave, but turned around one last time. "Hey kid," he said, tracing the bridge of his nose with his forefinger. "It won't scar."

The kid smiled slightly, and Josh couldn't help but smile back. Then, finally, he turned and ran.

* * *

Josh was sitting in an old Italian bar, one where as a kid he'd always seen old Italian men with two-day beards staggering out drunk and smelly. He knew that nobody there could possibly know him, not that it mattered. It was so dark inside that it took him a while for his vision to adjust. Besides, he too had a two-day beard and was working on getting just as drunk as he possibly could; he blended into his surroundings perfectly.

He was sitting by himself in a booth near the back of the bar. He didn't want to pass out, because he still had a loaded gun in his pocket. He wasn't exactly sure how he'd managed to hold on to it, but he could feel its weight pulling the coat to one side. Someone came through the front doors and Josh glanced up nervously, but the sunlight from outside was so bright that it was like being stabbed in the eyes. He was still rubbing his eyes and blinking away phantoms when he felt someone sit down across from him.

Josh looked up and found *The Man*.

He sat there for a moment clearly enjoying Josh's shock and recognition. He was dressed all in black, black hair flecked with gray spraying across his wrinkled fifty-year-old face and across one eye like crosshairs. He was exactly as he looked in Josh's dreams, and damned near what Josh though he himself might look like in twenty years. "I told you you'd see me again."

Josh was surprised to find that he felt no fear at all, no panicked need to get away. For the first time in his life, The Man felt more like… like *family*.

"You did good," The Man said with a voice that betrayed many years of smoking and whisky straight up. "I killed two of 'em." he rasped. He reached across and lifted Josh's drink in a silent toast to the sky and tipped it back. He set the remainder down in front of Josh with a pronounced *clack*. "You only killed one.'

"Who are you?" Josh slurred. The Man ignored him.

"I pity the bastard who saved me. He took down *four*. We seem to be working backwards geometrically."

Josh laughed. "You must've done good in math class too."

The Man laughed, a bark alien yet familiar. "Yeah. But where's that leave the new kid?"

Josh wrestled with that a moment, then returned to the figure swimming across from him. "Please," he stammered, fighting for coherency, "who are you? Are you *me*?"

"You? Heh." He smiled. "Nah. I'm not you, just like you're not the kid back there. But we're all… ah, what's a good word? Related? Connected? It's complicated." He laughed again, but only to himself. "You'll understand eventually. Maybe someday, we'll *all* understand." Then he slid out of the booth and walked over to the bar, handed the bartender something that made him very happy, then vanished out the front door in a flash of glare.

Josh sat staring at the door for some time. Eventually the bartender came over, sat another drink on the table in front of him and said; "Last call. Don't worry about your bill, your friend's got you covered."

Josh didn't doubt it.

Four

Stroke of Luck

Nobody was surprised that he'd been killed by lightning out of a clear blue sky. Gilbert had that kind of luck.

"Someone else is getting all my luck", he stated with absolute certainty. "I've always known it. I can feel it."

Gil attempted to prove it statistically by flipping a quarter over and over. It came up heads exactly 50% of the time. "Of course", he said dejectedly. "There's nothing at stake. I don't really win or lose either way."

He finally came up with a way to settle the matter once and for all. He purchased a revolver with six chambers and loaded a bullet into every other hole. He spun the cylinder and raised the gun to his temple.

"Fifty-fifty chance" he muttered. "And if I lose, at least that bastard out there won't be getting my luck anymore." He clenched his teeth and prepared to pull the trigger.

That was when the lightning struck. Witnesses said it came from nowhere, and seemed to aim directly for Gilbert's window. As for his experiment, it could only be called a draw. The cylinder had stopped on an empty chamber, but all three shells had been detonated by the lighting.

* * *

Everyone was shocked when Darren was run over by a bus and killed. He had always been the luckiest person they'd ever known.

Five

Homecoming

The blood red sun lay defeated on the horizon, throwing long cactus shadows Eastward across the desert floor, like accusing fingers pointed at the approaching darkness. Selena Fallon worked quickly in the failing light, her once delicate fingers removing clothespins from the line, and letting the freshly washed clothes drop into her basket.

"They sure don't take long to dry" she said wistfully, more to herself than her companion.

"Should they?" Missy Dearborn was taking her own clothes off the line.

"Back home in Louisiana, we'd hang up the washing in the morning, then have to wait 'til almost sunset before they'd be dry."

Missy smiled. "Here in Badwater it seems that by the time you finish hanging the last of the clothes, you got to start taking down the first clothes ya hung before they get sandblasted into threads."

Missy looked up. Selena had stopped working and was staring off into the distance, watching the sun disappear behind the mountains. "Yer thinking about yer husband, ain'tcha." Selena nodded slightly, her eyes heavy. "How long's it been?"

"Almost a year." She dabbed her eyes on her sleeve. "Seems longer though. Gavin joined the Army just after we got married. They transferred him to Fort Hannah when things started heating up with the Indians."

Missy continued plucking clothespins. "My daddy was in the Army. I think I saw him two weeks out of every year, usually at Christmas time. My momma said that sometimes she felt like a widow." Selena nodded again without looking up. "You must really be looking forward to seeing him tomorrow."

Selena only shrugged. Missy stopped and put her fists on her ample hips. "You don't look too excited about it. What's the matter."

"I'm scared."

"What for? He's still your husband."

"I'm scared he won't come."

"Don't you fret. Of course he'll come."

"And if he does, I... I might not know what to say to him."

Missy put her hands on Selena's shoulders. "Take it from someone who's been through it. The words'll come. The moment yer looking in his eyes it'll seem like he's never been gone. The hard part will be saying everything you want to say before he's gotta go back."

Selena looked up. "That's the other thing. It seems like we won't really have enough time! It's almost worse than not seeing him at all."

Missy smiled gently. "Yer wrong, honey. Yeah, it'll be too short. It feels like it goes by in a heartbeat. But you'll treasure each stolen moment as you get older. Trust me. Since my Derek died, I keep myself warm at night with the memories of every second we were able to spend together."

Selena attempted a smile and returned to the clothesline, but her thoughts remained dark and troubled.

* * *

Reverend Hightower emerged from around a corner into Selena's path, and she nearly ploughed straight into him. Behind his back, many of Badwater's children called him "God's Scarecrow". Though she would never say so aloud, Selena found it amusingly accurate. He was very tall and skeletally thin. His slicked back hair was as black and oily as the feathers of a raven. She had never seen him wear anything but a fine black suit, which he maintained so carefully that it always looked new. But it was his eyes that shook Selena; dark deep-set pits of scorn that scanned his congregation like he could see clean through to each man, woman and child's heart and whatever sin may lie there. He smiled with firmly closed lips as he brought that measuring stare to bear on her.

"Evenin' Mrs. Fallon." He said, flicking a dangling forelock with two fingers in lieu of tipping a hat.

"Evenin' Reverend." Selena wondered if she were trembling visibly. "Have you seen Doc around?"

"I just came from there. I'm afraid we lost poor Ned Kelly this afternoon."

"I'm sorry to hear that."

He shook his head slightly. "He was gettin' on in years, and the heat these last few days took whatever he had left. He's gone on to greener pastures." The Reverend looked up at the sky and scowled. "New moon tonight. It's gonna get mighty dark. You better get moving so you get home before you lose the light." He nodded a farewell and continued down the street. Selena smiled politely until he had gone a few paces, and then hurried the other direction.

* * *

Doc Jacobs answered the door wearing a blood stained butcher's apron. "Why howdy, Selena. What can I do for you?"

She smiled demurely, trying not to look at the stains. "I'm sorry to bother you this late, but I really need to talk to you. Can I come in?"

He squirmed uncomfortably, shooting a glance back over his shoulder. "It's not really a good time."

"Mr. Kelly?"

"Uh, yeah, actually. how'd you know that?"

"I ran into the Reverend on the way here."

He squinted his eyes. "Well, I'm afraid the smell is pretty strong in here. Not fittin' for a lady like yourself."

"Is there somewhere else we could go? It's very important."

He sighed heavily, glancing back into the room again. "Let me cover Ned up, and I'll walk you home."

Selena nodded and Doc withdrew into his shop.

He returned a moment later, no longer wearing the apron. He held an oil lantern in one hand, and extended the other elbow. Selena took his arm and he led her slowly down the street.

At first neither of them spoke, as if the hot silence of the evening were too thick to break. But finally, Doc's voice was strong enough to punch through. "So what seems to be the trouble, Selena. Is it about tomorrow?"

"Yes. I feel a little silly bringing it up, but I'm concerned about the Indians."

"What about 'em?"

"I'm afraid they'll stop Gavin from coming into town."

"How come?

"Because he's a soldier. I know that they're not the tribe that he was fighting, but the last time I talked to him, he was telling me how most Indians were starting to band together against whites."

Doc furled his brow. "That's true enough. But we've got something of an understanding with the local Injuns."

"I know."

"Ah." he said, tilting his head back slightly as understanding took root. "You think I could talk to 'em."

Selena looked down embarrassed. "I figured if anyone could, it would be you."

He smiled slightly, though it was hard to tell through his thick, unruly beard. "I'm probably as close to the Injuns as anyone in town is, but that's still not very close. I don't speak much Miwok, and the old medicine man ain't much better with English."

"But you *do* talk to him, don't you?"

"We generally get our meaning across, eventually. But we don't discuss much beyond cemetery business."

"Because we let them use our cemetery?"

"It's the other way around. We use *their* cemetery. They've been laying their dead to rest there for God knows how long. It's holy ground to them. The fact that they let us share it with them is unheard of. Badwater is probably the only place in the whole country where white folk bury their dead alongside the Injuns. It's created a bond between them and the town."

The last glowing embers of the desert sky went out as they arrived at Selena's door, leaving only the lantern glow to stave off complete blindness.

"You will talk to them, won't you?" she pleaded.

"I dunno. It's touchy. Part of the reason they get along with us so well is because we haven't gotten involved with the army none."

"You know as well as I do that Gavin – well, he didn't do anything he wasn't ordered to do…"

Doc put his enormous hands on her shoulders. "I'll talk to them. I can't make any promises. Nobody knows what Injuns think. Every time I think I've finally got 'em figured out, they go and do something different because some spirit animal told 'em to." Selena sighed heavily, holding back tears as Doc stroked her hair. "Don't fret now. You go inside and get a good night's sleep. I've got to go get Ned settled in, and I'll put in a word for Gavin when we're done."

Selena hugged him. "I can't ask more than that. Thanks, Doc." She released the big man and retreated into her house. Doc stared at the door a moment, then strode off into the oppressive night.

* * *

The street rippled and shimmered with heat ghosts dancing in the midday son. Despite the frying pan heat, most of the town was turned out, dressed in their Sunday finest and taking shelter from the sun under awnings and parasols. Sarah had opened the saloon early on account of the festivities, and was doing a rousing trade in a rare batch of oat beer.

Selena scanned the gathering nervously, but managed a smile and a curtsy for anyone she met. She finally found Doc kneeling on the porch of the Saloon, talking to Sarah's 13 year old son, Dusk. Doc was holding his fists in the air, moving one around the other like someone boxing, but really slowly.

"...but all that's really goin' on is that the moon is goin' in front of the sun, and blocks the light until it passes." Doc glanced up and noticed Selena approaching. Dusk continued staring at Doc's fists, envisioning the do-si-do of celestial spheres.

"Afternoon, Selena."

"Afternoon, Doc."

Dusk shot a glance up at the newcomer. "Howdy Mrs. Fallon" he mumbled, still chewing on ideas. "Hey Doc, how come it doesn't happen *every* new moon?"

Doc smiled. "It's kinda complex. Tell ya what, you swing by my place afterwards and I'll tell ya all about it." He tousled the boy's hair. "Yer mom gonna come out and watch?"

 "Nah", said the boy, "She says there's no reason to. She says she's seen the dark." He trotted into the saloon.

Doc stood up and brushed most of the dust off his knees. "Well, I talked to 'em, just like I said."

Selena tried desperately to read his expression. "And...?"

"And, they say they won't do nothin' to stop Gavin from coming into town."

The tension on Selena's face broke into a relieved smile, and she threw her arms around him. "Thank you so much, Doc, I can't tell you..."

Doc held her back at arms length, still quite serious. Selena's smile fell. "I said they'll do nothin'. They won't help him none either."

She shook her head. "I don't understand. Why would he need help?"

"They say he's still accountable for any wrongs he's done. Not to them, but to their spirits."

A cold breath went up her neck, setting all the hairs on her arms standing straight up. "What's to keep them from stopping Gavin and say their spirits did it?"

"They gave me their word, and they take that more seriously than most white folks I ever met. If they say they won't lift a finger against your husband, then they won't. But they won't lift a finger to protect him neither. That was the best I could do for you. I'm sorry."

Selena drew herself up, summoning a mask of cheerfulness. "Then that will have to do. Thank you for doing what you could."

Doc nodded, and sauntered into the saloon to see if there was any beer left.

* * *

"It's starting!" somebody yelled. Selena shielded her eyes, glancing at the sun between barely splayed fingers. Sure enough, the right side was beginning to dimple in. She'd heard that you weren't supposed to look directly at sun even during an eclipse, but she figured it couldn't be any worse than living in the glare of this God-forsaken desert year round. Sun blindness was a possibility that everyone in Badwater faced. Old Ned Kelly had been as blind as a bat when he died, and that was more common than not.

The sky grew blood red as the moon continued to devour the sun. A light breeze kicked up as if the hard pack was sighing with relief at the unexpected shade. Stars begin to show against the darkening sky, nightfall descending upon them mid day. Everyone in town milled about, craning their necks up at the heavens, and gawking at each other in the eerie dim glow that painted everything red.

Someone on the edge of town shouted, and everyone begin heading that way. A single star seemed to have fallen from the sky and lay twinkling on the ground. Out in the desert, someone had built a large fire. Selena didn't need to see the road to know that the fire was at the cemetery.

A hush fell over the gathering as they stopped between the last two buildings that defined Badwater in that direction, adamant about not crossing the imaginary line that separated "home" from *the desert*.

More lights were erupting into view, smaller fires being lit at intervals on either side of the road leading to town. Over the whispering of the breeze and her neighbors, Selena was beginning to hear a rhythmic sound. Drums. Chanting. Bells. The more she stared, the more she was sure she was seeing motion between the shimmering lights. And that motion, like the chanting, was getting closer.

The procession of Miwok drove straight toward the town, twirling and shuffling by torchlight, their chanting growing in volume and intensity. Every few yards, two decorated dancers would spin out of the crowd, stopping to light a cow skull lamp, place it at either edge of the road, then fall back into the frenetic ranks. Selena couldn't quite make out exactly how many their were, but there were *a lot* of them.

Selena about jumped out of her skin when someone touched her on the shoulder. She whipped around to find an Indian and almost screamed, then realized that it was Doc, all done up like a Miwok. Selena started to scold him, but Doc silenced her with two fingers placed lightly on her lips. His demeanor was solemn, and he nodded at her – perhaps to say "good luck", then pushed past her to the front of the gathering.

He emerged from the townspeople and walked a few paces down the road, then stopped and waited. The revelers approached, then prompted by some unseen signal, all stopped and fell silent with one last unified beat from the drummers, a period at the end of a sentence.

The Miwok medicine man embraced Doc and began speaking in his own language, but the tone was clearly ceremonial. When he stopped, Doc turned and faced Badwater and took a deep breath.

"As it has been since the world was created, the spirits look after us and guide us in our lives and our dealings with the Earth Mother. They surround us and comfort us when the winter is hard, they give us the strength to go on when the rains do not come. They laugh with us when the rains do come, and the soft grass claws its way through the desert floor."

Doc glanced back, and the old medicine man nodded.

"When Coyote steals the sun and hides it in his den, we return the embrace."

The Miwok parted, stepping off of the road to form a row on either side, holding their torches in front of them. Doc and the Indian mystic took the front position on opposite sides of the road and waited...

...and another group of people emerged from the darkness into the glow of the torchlight gauntlet. They came forward hesitantly at first, as if lost. As they spied the waiting townfolk, they entered the town more confidently, led foremost by Old Ned Kelly.

People began rushing forward as they spotted their loved ones. Husbands and wives, sons and daughters, parents, grandparents, great grandparents, reunited momentarily in excited embraces, then hurrying off to quieter corners. Whole families gathered together in clumps, crying and laughing, or just holding hands silently. Ned's widow ran to him, and he picked her up and span around in jubilation. Missy Dearborn spotted her husband Derek among the travelers, and sprinted to him, holding up the hem of her skirts. They fell into a passionate embrace.

Selena scanned the crowd frantically. The last few stragglers were clear of the twin columns of Indians. She waited a moment longer, until she was sure there were no more. Her heart fell, and rage swelled in her. She launched herself at the Medicine man.

"You BASTARD!! She screamed, pounding his decorated chest with her fists. Doc immediately grabbed her wrists and pulled her off, restraining her easily.

"Stop it, Selena. This isn't right".

"Isn't right?! These godless savages have done something to Gavin!"

The medicine man adjusted his beads and feathers back into order, and drew himself up. "We did not stop him from crossing the river of death. He did not come. Not everyone can."

"What do you mean?" Selena sobbed. "Why can't Gavin come?"

The old Indian said something in Miwok. Doc nodded seriously. "Selena, why don't I take you home. Gavin won't be here today."

"But we put him in the cemetery just like you said! His parents wanted to give him a proper Christian burial in New Orleans, but you promised he'd be able to come back if we did it *their* way."

"I didn't promise anything, Selena."

"They killed him, and now they won't even let him visit." She buried her face in Doc's robes, her body wracked with sobbing. Doc exchanged glances with the medicine man, who merely shook his head, then glanced up at the sky. A shard of light was beginning to emerge from behind the moon.

Selena finally mustered enough composure to stand on her own. She pulled away from Doc to realize that she was no longer the only one crying. The dead were gone, and the Miwok were already beginning to file back out into the rapidly brightening desert. Likewise, the good people of Badwater began to compose themselves enough to return to their normal daily lives.

Doc walked Selena home, and by the time they reached her door, it was broad daylight again, the desert heat wrapping around them like a stifling but somehow comforting blanket, evaporating any tears that still spilled from Selena's eyes.

"Doc?"

"Yes, Selena?"

"Was my Husband an evil man?"

"No. Gavin was a good man."

"Then why couldn't he come?"

"I don't know, Selena. There's a lot about this whole business I don't understand. I don't think even the Injuns know the whole deal. I do know that at some point in his life, damn near every man has to do something he wishes he didn't have to do. I recon we make our choices and then have to live with the consequences."

Selena opened her door and stepped in, stopping in the threshold without turning around. "I'm never going to see him again, am I?"

Doc gazed at Selena's back. Even from behind she was beginning to show the wear of too many years in the desert. "Most folks don't *ever* get to see their dead again."

"They do around here."

"I'm sorry, Selena."

She disappeared into her dark, quiet home and closed the door.

Six

Altruism

Our founding fathers were more farsighted than seems possible, even in light of the powers they harnessed. The things that they could do that seem so much like magic that one must constantly remind themselves that they were once even more primitive than we are now.

Before the crash, they could even fly. They had machines that could think and talk just like another person. Their cities towered over the highest trees - even bigger than some mountains, and were so strong that the skeletal remains still stand. As I say, this was before the crash.

No one really knows what happened. It's been so long that no one who was there still lives. We have folk legends of living spirits that swirled through the air, strangling all those who were caught out in the open. Some of the legends say that even these spirits were created by the men of those times, and that they got out of control and laid waste even the lands of their masters. Anyway, they all died practically overnight. Most of the survivors were in the lands far from the cities, in the farms and wooded areas. For years, those that survived were afraid to go near the cities, in case the spirits still roamed the streets looking for victims.

In the country, it seemed the spirits preferred animals. The cows wasted away and died, the forest animals were found dead by the thousands. Anyone who ate one of the animals died too.

When I was just a kid, they were still growing grain in huge fields that waved in the wind like some golden lake. Then the ground dried up, and now you can only find small patches of dirt here and there that can grow anything. Then you've got to hold it. There just ain't enough patches of good dirt to grow enough for everyone, so others try and take it from you. My brother died keeping us alive. He volunteered for it, as many did. It's considered a great honor to die so that the rest can eat. I knew it was a matter of time before all the men got picked off, then the crop and the women would be up for grabs.

I figured that the people who built them cities must have been smart enough to know what to do about this, if they were still around. I also didn't believe that those old spirits were still around, and besides, I could run faster than anyone I knew. I set out one morning to find an answer to our prayers from the fathers.

I was terrified as I walked the broken rock road, which was so wide eight carts could have gone down it side by side. If I died this far from home, no one would be helped. Still, I pressed on into the wreckage which sprang up from the desert floor like vast rusting cacti.

When the towers closed around me like a box canyon, I stopped. The roads were buried under the fallen skins of the buildings, broken glass was everywhere. Everything was deathly still except for the wind blowing through the bones of the city. Sometimes I would think I heard whispering, but when I would cock my head to listen, there was only more wind. I felt vulnerable out in the open, so I moved closer to the nearest wall. Rubble was piled high against it in snow-like drifts I could only guess how deep. They were at least high enough so that I could climb them and look in through the broken windows.

Inside was a room, with a huge table and the biggest chair I'd ever seen. By the way they were arranged, it looked like whoever lived here ate by themselves. The thought of food made me think that there must be a kitchen nearby, and while there was certainly not going to be any food, there would be pots and pans, and maybe knives. I thought Momma could certainly use those. I carefully broke enough glass out of the window frame and climbed through.

The air smelled like dust and mold. I waited a moment, listening, but nothing stirred. Looking at the table, I found that the side towards the chair had huge drawers in it. I looked inside, and mostly found papers and little gizmos of twisted wires. There were pencils too, and I grabbed these for old Hubey who can read and write some. Then I went to the door. It opened just like it was new.

The room beyond must have been some kind of dining room, but every table had only one chair, and they all had little walls around them so that no one could see each other while they were eating. I had to wonder when they talked to each other, if not at dinner. Then I remembered a story my grandpa had told me about the fathers being able to talk to each other even when they weren't in the same place.

I slowly wandered through the room, looking for anything that might lead me to the kitchen. Almost every table had stacks and stacks of papers and pencils, But I already had more than old Hubey would ever be able to use in his life. I also kept finding little snake-head-shaped-things with sharp teeth like a viper and by squeezing it, it would bite. I figured that the fathers used 'em like forks.

Then I heard the noise. It was a quiet hum like a bee, but softer. I froze, then started lookin' for where it was comin' from. Then I found the hole.

A huge section of the floor had given away, and there was another room underneath the dining room. A couple of the little tables had fallen through and were smashed on the floor below. And around them – Cooking stuff!

I dropped to my hands and knees and looked down. The humming sound was definitely coming from down here, and all around was a weirder kitchen than I'd ever imagined. Rows and rows of cooking pots and jars of every size and shape. I brought my head as low to the ground as I could, trying to peer into the dark chamber. Suddenly, the floor broke with a loud crack and I tumbled off into the hole. I shouted and grabbed out for, well, anything. What I got was a clump of cords that stuck out of the floor. They held my weight and were so long that they almost reached the floor below. I shimmied down low enough to drop. The table I landed on shifted in the mound, but didn't tip over. Soon my footsteps were echoing off the hard smooth floor.

I shouted again as the room was suddenly filled with light! I spun around terrified, but there was no one there but me. The light came from windows in the ceiling, but I could see through the hole that the room above was still dark. I murmured a prayer of protection against the spirits, and looked around.

The kitchen was a sparkling wonderland of glass and metal so shiny I could see my face in it. So many jars and bottles, some with little curly tubes going from one to another, some with labels which meant nothing to me. There were little boxes with windows in the front, but I couldn't see anything inside them, and in front of those were trays of square pegs, each one with a letter on it. It was all so strange that I was beginning to wonder if I *had* found the kitchen, but then I found a couple of tiny burners. I had to wonder how they cooked enough food for all the people at the tables upstairs. There were certainly enough pots and things, but only one or two burners.

I finally worked up the nerve to go over to the far end of the kitchen, where there was the biggest door I'd ever seen. Standing right in front of it, I could hear the humming sound better than ever and I could feel a kind of buzzing when I put my hand on it. And it was cold! I ran my hand along it, amazed that it could be so cold. There was a huge lever on the door, and I pulled on it just to see if it would move. It wouldn't at first, so I pulled harder. With a great cracking sound, the door opened, and winter poured out. Great swirls of white clouds rushed out, and I ran, thinking it was the spirits, but I wasn't fast enough, and soon I was engulfed in a freezing mist. I held my breath as long as I could, then gave out and prepared to die.

I didn't die, and the clouds faded, and I was left alone, shivering in the cold. I looked into the room beyond the big door. It blazed with light and was covered in ice and snow. Even though I hadn't brought a coat, I couldn't turn away now, so I approached the door. Inside was a seemingly endless tunnel of shelves, all draped heavily with icicles. There were some huge, fur lined coats hung on pegs inside the door, so I shook one off and put it on. Within moments, the chill was bearable, and I went deeper into the chamber.

The walls were lined with shelves from floor to ceiling, well over my head. On each shelf was a glass case. I went over to the nearest one and chipped away at the curtain of frost that had built up on it. Eventually, I could see what treasure lie inside.

Meat.

Perfectly frozen and preserved meat.

Enough meat on these shelves to feed thousands of people, possible for years.

I closed the big heavy door carefully, making sure it latched. I piled up the tables that had fallen into the kitchen until I could climb back up through the hole. I ran all the way back to the camp so hard that when I got back it was a full half hour before I could talk, and could barely walk for several days. They carried me when I showed a big group of men with ropes how to get to the kitchen. Old Hubey came with us since he was the only one who could still read some. He would read signs and papers, then wouldn't say anything for a long time. He kept saying that everything was O.K., but something was bugging him. He said that the meat should be just fine, even after all this time.

The fathers had left it for us. They must have somehow known that the spirits were coming, and that we'd all be hungry someday. And they volunteered. Just like my brother. Even back then it was an honor to die so that other could eat. They volunteered by the thousands, and used some of their best magic and science and built an entire building so that the meat would still be good even after all these years.

Old Hubey said the place was called *cryogenics*. He says it just means a cold place.

Seven

Conjunction of Solitude

Maximillian Jordan's eyes were fixed on the horizon, his breath making pulsing ghosts dance on the near-frozen glass. He checked a chart, making certain he was staring at the right place on the rusted lip of the volcanic crater he sat in. The sky was beginning to glow with the palest shade of pink, anticipating the tardy sunrise. It was forty minutes late, as usual. Days on Mars just didn't have the frantic pace they did back home on Earth.

As if on cue, a brilliant point of light ignited on a small rise, then lifted lazily upward, with the light came the memory of noise; traffic choked streets, crowds of voices, babies crying, phones ringing, all the din and cacophony that Max associated with the distant blue world. It was visible for but a moment, then a pool of molten gold welled up on the horizon, shimmering a moment as through threatening to flow down the cliffs and fill the caldera of Arisa Mons. It rose instead to pursue the Earth and consume it in glare. The sun appeared smaller and dimmer from Mars, but was still bright enough to cause the viewports of the landing craft Keener to tint themselves in protest.

A tiny voice squeaked from the communications headset resting on the control console. Max stared at it a moment, disappointed by the theft of his privacy. The voice spoke again, too quiet to be intelligible, yet still betraying an air of tension or anxiety. Sighing with resignation, he donned the headset as delicately as one might a wreath of laurels.

"Max, come in please! Do you read!?"

"Roger, Chris, I copy."

"It's about time! Everything o.k.?"

"Affirmative. Sorry about that"

"Hey, no problem. It's just my life out here."

"I said I'm sorry." Max rubbed his temples. "So what's up?"

Chris sounded immediately more at ease. "I've got the seismographic package set up. You should be getting a signal."

Max punched a code into his computer keyboard, and a screen flared into a display of dancing lines. "Check, seismograph transmitting nice and clear."

"Lovely. I'm coming back in then."

"Roger, see you in a bit."

He closed the channel and returned his gaze outward,, savoring the last few minutes of silence. It lasted a mere fleeting moment, then was shattered by throbbing machinery and loud hissing from the lower deck as the airlock cycled, without looking away from the viewport. Max listened to the whine of the airlock door opening, followed by the unmistakable rustle of someone doffing a pressure suit.

Suddenly, Chris Delaney shot from the hatch to the flight deck, alighting on its lip. Even in Mars' gravity, two-fifths that of Earth, this was quite a leap. He ran his fingers across his crew cut, looking irritated.

"That wasn't funny."

"What?"

"Leaving me alone out there like that."

"Oh. Wasn't meant to be. Just wasn't paying attention." Max sighed. "It was unprofessional of *me,* and I apologize."

Chris seemed satisfied. "It's o.k., it just makes me a little nervous to be on the surface with no..."

"...Lifeline?" Max interrupted, smirking.

"Well, yes. I suppose. "

Max smiled. "That's understandable. I'm probably crazy for not feeling that way."

Chris looked up, also smiling. The two had learned to appreciate each other's differences, a skill essential for people who were locked into a tiny vehicle for 14 months together.

Max flinched as a burst of static startled them. The noise sorted itself into a distant-sounding voice.

"Uh, Kepler, this is Copernicus, do you copy?"

Chris touched a switch on the console. "Roger, Copernicus, We read loud and clear. It's good to hear your voice!"

"Aw, How sweet!" Muffled laughter drifted out of the background noise. Chris was not amused, his comment had been more sincere than his crewmates in orbit had realized. "We thought we'd check in and see if you had any last messages for Houston before the Earth falls into the sun."

Max and Chris looked at each other, shaking their heads. Neither one had spouses to send word to, and had had their fill of answering media questions during the first interplanetary press conference two days after landing and all the hoopla and pageantry that came with it.

"Hey, I know!" Max exclaimed. "Tell them to send up room service with a bottle of champagne!"

Again, laughter from high above. "Roger, Kepler, but I wouldn't hold my breath. It'll be two days before the Earth comes out from behind the sun."

A liquid shiver flowed down the back of Chris' neck. Two days?! It was bad enough being so far removed from the rest of humanity that it took ten minutes for a message to get to mission control and another ten minutes to receive a reply. The thought of total radio blackout bothered him, even though he had known this would happen from the beginning. "Understood Copernicus, Kepler out. "

Max leaned back in his chair, yawning and stretching. "You know, Chris, Mars would have been a great place to hide."

"What do you mean?"

"Didn't you ever play 'hide-and-seek' as a kid?"

"Not when I could avoid it." He looked at his feet. "I was always 'it' "

"I did, every chance I got. But after a while, no one would let me play."

"Why's that?"

Max smiled. "I was too good at hiding. I knew all the best spots. I'd hide somewhere cozy, bathed in sunshine with a good view of the sky, and just lie there and daydream. They could never find me, and I never came out — not even when they called 'olly-oxen'.

Eventually, the other kids would give up looking, and I might hide until dark. My mom quit worrying after the first few times."

Chris was obviously uncomfortable with the idea. "Didn't you get bored? Or lonely?"

"Nah. I grew up in a big family in a small house. Most of my childhood I shared a bed with two brothers. Sometimes I'd get to feeling so crowded I would pull all of my toys out of my toy box, crawl inside and shut the lid. Sometimes I'd lie there for hours, no light, no sound, no hassles. Perfect isolation." He smiled with fond remembrance,, his attention drifting out the viewport. "But this," he motioned to the rusted landscape, "this is better."

* * *

The following evening, Chris lay in his bunk. The soft breathing of the air scrubbers was soothing, and his mind began to drift among the stars he was surrounded by.

He always detested hide-and-seek. He was forever seeking, never hiding, when he did hide, he always felt the other kids didn't look for him. Once, he covered his eyes and counted to twenty-five. "Ready or not, here I come!" the neighborhood children were nowhere to be found. He searched thoroughly, in every possible spot, some twice or three times, then gave up, returning home in tears. Later he found out that they had all ran off together to the local market for candy and soda, quite amused at having ditched him.

* * *

Chris slept very uneasily that night. In his dreams, the Earth fell into the sun with a tremendous molten splash, burning to a cinder instantly. He sat in orbit aboard a tiny spacecraft, staring out a window at the death of his home world. He screamed violently but with no sound, and then turned to find there was no one else on board.

The two astronauts got an early start the next morning, busying themselves with their scheduled routine of electronic surveillance and research, coupled with observations from Copernicus. After lunch. Max and Chris left the safety of the lander to scout about, collecting rocks and soil samples to be analyzed on Earth, and deploying various scientific instruments that would send their findings across the void for years to come.

After six hours they returned to Kepler, settling down to paperwork and general housekeeping. The western sky was blazing with the reds of the sunset when their skyward comrades next signaled.

"Kepler, we have lost all contact with the meteorological station you guys set up yesterday."

"Damn." Max muttered. This was one of the most crucial experiments the mission would install, constantly monitoring Mars' weather cycles. "Any idea what happened?"

"Negative. Could have been hit by a meteorite, or the antenna might simply have blown over. We do have a lot of meteor activity going on up here."

"I bet you want us to go EVA and check it out."

"You got it. Let us know what you find out. Copernicus out."

Max stood. "Guess it's my turn to go for a walk."

Chris winced. "Be careful out there, its getting dark."

"O.k. mom. Should I wear a coat?"

Chris ignored the sarcasm. "Just keep your eyes open, all right? You'll be alone out there."

Max was already halfway through the hatch to the lower deck. "And you'll be alone in here."

He dropped below the floor, leaving the air as still and tense as a morgue. Chris switched on the exterior floodlights, and watched as Max emerged from below, waved, and headed away from the ship. Gradually, the white-suited figure made his way up the slope, paused momentarily at the crest, and then sank down the other side.

* * *

Matthew Delaney was a sophomore in college, a promising engineering student, Chris' older brother and closest friend. In spite of the difference in their years, Chris then a junior in high school, the two brothers spent a great deal of time together. One day Matt left for a weekend in the mountains. A logging truck coming down the mountain lost its brakes and careened over a ravine, taking Mail's car with it. There were no survivors.

* * *

Hours passed slowly and silently. Chris-began to wonder if he should check in with Max, his concern growing with each minute, but did not want to intrude on his valued privacy.

Without warning, his ears were stabbed with sharp static. Slapping the earphones off his head, he lowered the volume, then picked the headset off of the floor, white noise raged, consuming the airwaves. Frantically, he adjusted the communications equipment, finding no traces of any of his companions.

"Copernicus, this is Kepler, Come in. "

There was no reply.

"Copernicus, this is Kepler, do you copy?"

Waves of static rolled on.

"Copernicus? Can you hear me?!"

Nothing.

He switched to the frequency where he should find Max, but again found only aural snow.

"Max, This is Chris, do you copy?"

The sound was that of a hundred snakes and carried no less menace.

"Max?"

* * *

Chris was eight. The family had spent a week camping at the lake, and his parents were loading the station wagon for the trip home. He sat in the back seat, busily arranging the pillows and rolled sleeping bags that towered over him into a little chamber he could sleep in during the long drive.

"Oh no!" he murmured, "the moon rock!" It wasn't really, of course, but the piece of granite he'd found did look like the pictures in his books. He hopped into the front seat, out the open door, and ran down the path to the campsite. He found his treasure where he'd left it in the now barren spot, right next to where the tent had been. He snatched it up, then whirled around, startled by the sound of the car starting. .

"WAIT!" he screamed, running back to the parking lot. "Mom! Dad!" He reached the road in time to see taillights receding in the distance. They drove for nearly an hour before discovering the absence of their son.

There were no taillights this, time, and home was 377,000,000 kilometers away.

* * *

Christopher Delaney's eyes were fixed on the horizon, his breath making pulsing ghosts dance on the near-frozen glass. He checked a chart, making certain he was staring at the right place on the rusted lip of the volcanic caldera he sat in. The sky was beginning to glow with the palest shade of pink, anticipating the tardy sunrise. It was forty minutes late as usual.

As he so dearly hoped, a brilliant point of light ignited on a small rise, then rose lazily upward. The ocean of static that he had been listening to all night began to take on some rhythm, then the patterns formed into words.

"Good morning, Kepler!" The voice was distorted, yet understandable.

"HA! Good morning! Where the hell have you been!?'" Chris screamed with joy, his voice haggard.

"It's a long story, but the jist of it is that we had our communications dish taken out by a nasty little meteor. We're all jury rigged now, but I'm afraid you'll still lose us every time we swing around the back side of the planet until we can get things fixed up a bit more. All in all, I'd say things could be a hell of a lot worse"

The point of light that was Copernicus rose fast enough to avoid the pursuing sun, behind which followed yet another glimmer, that which Chris knew to be his home world. He laughed long and hard until tears ran down his cheeks.

"I'll second that, Copernicus, things could be much worse."

A third point of light appeared on the horizon, dropping slowly down the cliffs towards the valley floor. It was Max, probably unaware that anything had happened, or that his radio was not being relayed from the orbiter.

Chris watched the spreading vertical stack of lights, awestruck by their symmetry, like some great conjunction of stars or planets. Suddenly he realized that for just a fleeting moment at dawn, everything in the universe that meant anything to him had aligned at a single point, just below the horizon, while he feared he would never see any of them again. A rush of warmth flooded through him, and somehow a realization came to him that he had never seen before. He had never really been alone in his life before this morning. How can one be alone on a world with billions of people?!

He wiped tears from his eyes, knowing with absolute certainty that he would never be alone again.

Eight
No Deposit, No Return

"Mike?"

There was no reply from the unconscious figure slumped in the chair. In fact, the only sounds that were audible were the faint trilling of the control board and the hypnotic, almost subliminal vibration of the ship's fusion reactors.

"Mike?"

Again there was no reply. Impatiently, Sherman leaned back and slammed his foot into his co-pilot's seat. Mike sprang suddenly upright with a look of mad terror strewn across his face, arms held up in defense against the unknown. He searched the room frantically for his assailant, then scowled angrily as he only found Sherm's idiotic grin. He sat still for a moment, letting the consciousness so rudely foisted upon him settle into his brain.

"Don't ever do that again unless the hull is breeched," he hissed through gritted teeth.

Sherman just smirked. "Take a look at this."

Mike rubbed his face with both hands, then leaned forward in his seat to gaze at the scanner. "What is it?"

"Not sure yet. Small metallic object just inside the next quadrant."

"You woke me up for *that*?" Mike snarled angrily. "It's probably just a trash container jettisoned by a passing ship."

"Uh uh. Not enough velocity."

"OK, so it's a meteor. Is it nickel or iron?"

"Steel, with heavy traces of aluminum and gold."

Mike blinked. "Aluminum? Are you sure?"

"Check it yourself."

Finally intrigued, Mike stood and came around behind Sherman's seat to get a better look at his readout screens. "Well, I'll be damned." Sherman sat a little taller as his boss realized the full implications.

"When are we expected by the Borland colony?"

Sherm smiled. "Four days from now. We're almost a full day ahead of schedule."

Mike nodded coolly and returned to his seat, his fingers darting over the smooth surface of the control panel. "OK, let's go see what you've found."

The freighter *Chesley Bonestell* pivoted gracefully on its center of mass and Mike throttled the engines up, swinging the ship in a long arc away from its previous course.

A few hours later, Mike swung the ship around to match the object's trajectory and velocity, then shut down the mighty fusion engines.

"Alright Sherm. It's your fish, you reel it in."

Sherman activated the cargo waldos, and gently plucked the vagrant instrument from the blackness of space with delicate metal fingers. He placed it into the light flooded airlock on the craft's belly.

"Hit it with the full decontamination protocol. We don't know where this thing has been."

Sherman scowled impatiently, but began flooding the airlock with anti-biological gasses.

Sherman bounded to the hatch, fidgeting excitedly as the airlock purged and repressurized. He slid between the doors as soon as they were open enough to squeeze through, his older companion following more leisurely.

"Hey! We got us an antique" Sherman said.

"Yeah, looks like it." Mike walked around it, assessing it carefully.

"Sure is in bad shape. Looks like it took a meteor strike there." Sherm pointed. "And look at this dish! How far do you think we'd be if we still used antennas like that?"

Mike snickered esoterically. "Not far enough," he whispered, a far-away sound in his voice.

Sherm raised an eyebrow. "What's the joke?"

"You don't recognize it?"

Sherm shook his head. "I know it's one of those old unmanned probes the government used to send out. I bet we can get some decent money for it if we take it to a museum on the return trip."

Mike frowned. "It's not just any probe." His knees creaked as he crouched to inspect the craft closer. "We weren't supposed to get this one back until *someone else* brought it back to us."

"Huh?"

"It's a *Voyager.* I'm afraid we've passed ourselves."

"So?"

"So, it's like putting a note in a bottle and throwing in into the ocean, hoping that someone else will find it, read it, and maybe send back a reply. Then one night, you're out walking along on a beach somewhere else, maybe even on the other side of the ocean, and you find the same bottle again, your note still inside, unread."

"Kinda funny, dontcha think?"

"Kinda sad. It was a nice idea."

Sherman shrugged. "It just sounds like they underestimated themselves."

"Yeah, maybe. I just can't help but be disappointed. Well, at least they were *trying*. If there *is* someone out there, we're bound to bump into them sooner or later."

"I guess. So what's the deal with the fancy plaque?"

Mike smiled softly and ran his fingers over the cryptic diagrams etched into the gold disc affixed to the side of the probe. "Greetings from Earth. There's an old-style record inside with messages from the governments of the time, music from all over the world, and a bunch of other sounds."

"Huh. Cool." Sherm paused a moment thoughtfully, then a grin lit up his face. Hey, you want to listen to it?"

Mike pondered it a moment, then slowly shook his head. "Nah, it wasn't meant for us. Besides, it's gonna be two years before we'll be back on Earth. It'll just make me homesick."

Nine

A Distant Baying

I slammed the door behind me, locking all the bastards out. Every anal retentive accountant, every back-biting manager, every whining client, all locked out of my life for another twelve hours. Christ on a stick, if I'd had to stay at the office another nanosecond, I'd have murdered someone with my stapler. But now I was safely locked inside my fortress of sanity, the madness of the working world waiting tangibly outside my door.

I took a deep breath, trying to force my shoulders to relax through sheer willpower. "Home", I thought to myself over and over. "It's all okay now, I'm home."

First, some music. Ah, yes. Mr. Brubeck should do the trick nicely. The CD slid into the player with only the slightest of whispers, and after a moment there was a jazz quintet playing live but unseen in my living room. Next order of business; a drink.

The players followed me into the kitchen. That always impressed my guests. Almost as much as when they found that there were even speakers in the bathroom. I'd come to wonder why no one else ever did the same thing. I guess I just take the quality of the music I listen to more seriously than most.

Cognac. Most definitely. I pulled out the snifter etched with my initials, the bottle of Remy V.V.S.O.P. gurgling lightly as I filled it halfway. The bottle was nearly empty, so I made a mental note to pick up another the next time I went shopping. Giving the glass a gentle twirl, I inhaled the delicious vapors that make cognac such a treat. "Wine is for drinking," I would often quip at parties, "Cognac is for snorting." I found the vulgarity of the phraseology amusing.

Still swirling my snifter, I strolled back into the den. The atmosphere was nearly complete. With the touch of a switch the fireplace blazed into golden light. I adjusted the dimmer switch to get the maximum effect from the fire, then settled slowly into my recliner. Yes. I sighed. This was perfect. I sipped gently at the cognac, feeling the silky burn glide across my tongue, listening to Dave and the boys caress my ears in 5/4 time.

Pounding like rhythmic thunder erupted from the door. Annoyed at the sheer gall of fate to interrupt this oh-so-badly-needed healing, I merely stared at the door without moving. There was a moment of silence, then the urgent pounding began again. "Son of a bitch," I thought, staring at the door in disbelief. No one had ever pounded on my door before. I thought that only happened in the movies. In real life, people knocked. Just to dispel any doubts, the someone pounded again.

For a split second, I considered simply ignoring the intruder until he gave up and went away. (He? I couldn't imagine a woman pounding so brutally like this.) However, my anger at the nerve of destroying such a fine mood overcame my patience, and I stormed out of my chair to let this idiot know just what I thought of this breach of human decency right to his face.

I played the usual guessing game as I ripped the door open, but I lost. Standing huddled in the porch light with kamikaze moths darting around his head was Frank Collins, a co- worker whom I occasionally lunched with. He was a mess, still wearing his suit from the office although it looked as though it had been through a war or two. His shirt was untucked and crooked, the knees of his trousers were ripped and stained. His eyes were bloodshot and darting around frantically. Then I suddenly remembered that he hadn't been seen at the office for three days.

"Frank?"

"Steve, uh, hi." He looked frantically over his shoulder. "Sorry it's so, uh, late. Can I, ah…" He gestured through the half opened door with his chin.

"Oh, ah, sure", I muttered, praying silently that this wouldn't take long. "Come in."

He practically backed through the door, pulling it tightly against himself, squeezing through the tiniest opening possible. He sighed loudly once the latch clicked closed behind him, his shoulders dropping with released tension.

Automatically, I slipped into host mode. "Can I fix you a drink?" He nodded almost imperceptibly. I went back to the kitchen and pulled a bottle of cheap bourbon out from under the sink. He didn't seem in a discriminatory frame of mind, and it didn't seem to me that he deserved much better. I started back towards the foyer, but stopped mid-stride and winced as the music was stopped with surgical precision between notes. I found him in the living room, holding the curtains aside with a finger and peering out the window into the night. He jerked around to face me as I came out of the kitchen, then relaxed when he saw that it was only me. He took the drink and downed it with a single gulp. I mentally gnashed my teeth with fury at this mutilation of a soothing evening while externally revealing nothing but concern for a friend in need. "Have a seat."

He fell into my chair, still nervously glancing occasionally towards the hallway. Somehow, his eyes found their way back to me and some twisted cousin to a smile crossed his face. "God," he snickered spasmodically, "I must be a sight."

I smiled. "Probably not the best time to ask the boss for a raise," I chuckled. The humor seemed to be lost on him.

We sat in silence as he gathered his composure. Just as I thought he might fall asleep in the chair he cleared his throat.

"You're not going to believe me."

I felt sure he was right. "Try me."

"It's wolves."

"Wolves."

He sat there staring at me as if this explained everything but I just wasn't getting it. Eventually he realized this and began.

"I saw the first one about three months ago. I was driving to work - just like any normal Thursday. I, I was thinking about the Benson account, and how to soften old man Simon up about letting me take him out to lunch at the Belmonte, when all of the sudden, out of the corner of my eye, I see this wolf."

"A wolf?"

"Yeah. A Wolf."

"What were you doing, driving to work via Colorado?"

"No!" he pleaded. "I was on North 38th street! Downtown! Thing is, when I turn my head to look at it, it isn't a wolf at all. It's a pile of trash up against a fire hydrant. It wasn't a wolf at all." He shuddered, somewhere between a sob and a laugh. "I didn't think much of it at the time, I had too much on my mind. About a week later, I saw another one.

"This time I was at home, and I was working on the deck. You know, Caroline and I have always wanted a deck around the back of the house, but 'til old man Simon comes through with a raise I can't afford a contractor, so I'm building it myself. Anyways, I'm hammering away and on the upswing, I see this dog in my peripheral vision. I froze, 'cause we don't have a dog and the yard is fenced. But when I turn around, there's just my old wheelbarrow, upside-down, just where I left it. Can I have another drink?"

It took me a second to realize that he's asked me a question, so I sat there with this expectant look on my face waiting for the next part of the story. Host mode finally kicked in and I jumped up for another bourbon, then sat down on the sofa. He sipped at it this time, then looked up at the ceiling as if trying to find where he left off.

"So you thought the wheelbarrow was a dog..." I prompt.

"Yeah," he continues, "so I see this dog, only every time the image comes back to me in retrospect, it's clearly your classic gray and white arctic-type wolf with the steely eyes and..."

His voice trailed off, and he again craned his neck to look back at the door.

"A wolf." I prompted.

"Yeah." He sipped at his drink. Then he nodded. "Yeah."

I waited. Finally, he drew in a breath and continued. "It got worse. Pretty soon I'm seeing them three, four times a day. Each time I'd catch this wolf out of the corner of my eye, but when I turn to look, it's just some old tires or a shadow. I thought sure that I was seeing wolves because, for whatever reason, I was lookin' for them. You know? I had wolves on the brain. I tried to just ignore it, figuring that if I thought about something else they would just go away.

"Sounds reasonable", I offered.

"Of course it does," he murmured. "You just don't see wolves in the suburbs."

"I hear that over in Moraga they occasionally get coyotes digging through people's garbage. Sometimes they even get deer on the golf course..."

"THIS IS DIFFERENT !!" he screamed. I was stunned into silence, my mouth working soundlessly as he dropped his face into his shaking hands. After a moment of tense silence he sobbed an nearly inaudible "I'm sorry" between his palms. We sat that way for a very long, uncomfortable time, with me wondering what the hell I was going to do. Finally, Frank quit shuddering, took a deep breath, then looked up again with an apologetic smile. "Jesus, I must sound crazy." he muttered.

"You're obviously very upset," I reassured. *As long as I'm on his side, he won't be dangerous.* My pulse was racing. I'd often looked at co-workers like black widows before; very dangerous, but as long as you recognized them and kept your distance... Frank was more like a hand grenade with the pin pulled. As long as you held onto the clip and handled it very carefully...

He regained his composure and continued. "They must have started getting braver. Last week, they let me see it happen." He took a deep breath. "I went to lunch by myself. That was that day you couldn't come because you were tying down the Markham account." I looked away briefly, I had lied to him about having work to do, but Davis had wanted to talk to me over crab salad at Salmagundie's, and he is Simon's right hand man....

"So I'm sitting at one of the tables outside that little sandwich shop, when I look up and see this wolf sittin' across the street.. This time I'm lookin' right at it, and it's real clear it's staring right at me. It just sits there a moment, staring like it's hungry, then all of the sudden it melts."

"It melts…"

"Yeah. It just… I dunno, it *melts*, kinda shimmers a bit, then there's nothin' there except a bit of hedge. Just this bush. I eat at this place every day. I almost always sit in the same place, and just stare off into space and, you know, think." I nod, even though I have no idea what he's babbling about. "I *know* there's no bush there."

I started wondering how I could tactfully turn him over to the appropriate authorities. I must have let some doubt show on my face, because he realized that he was losing me.

"Look, it's like this", he sputtered, holding his palms toward me as if trying to convince me to hold off passing judgment on him. " I don't know why, but they quit hiding from me," he stammered urgently. "Maybe they felt they were so close they didn't need to hide anymore. Hell, this morning I thought I'd try going in to the office, maybe take some paperwork to do at home, and halfway through the business park I realized they were trotting alongside the car. Ten or twelve of them." His shaking began with renewed intensity.

"Frank, I…"

He interrupted, speaking very fast. " I looked 'wolf' up in he encyclopedia Sharon and I bought for our son. Do you know what they do?"

I shook my head. *Keep him talking.*

"They follow a herd of antelope or water buffalo or whatever. When one of the herd gets so old or sick or fat that they can't keep up, they fall behind. If they get too far behind, the herd can't protect them. The wolf pack singles the straggler out." He started looking at the door again. "They surround him. Then, they rip him to shreds,"

"Frank," I said with a soothing smile. "You aren't a water buffalo."

"WELL WHAT THE HELL AM I?! He exploded. "WHAT THE HELL ARE YOU ?!

I cringed, pressing my back deep into the sofa and looking around for something that might serve as a weapon just in case it should come to that. Nothing looked promising for even an improvised club.

"We're, uh, we're people", I stammered, praying that at least this much was obvious to him. "We are human beings."

"Yes, yes. We are humans, just like any elk is an elk. But what do we do for the herd ?"

"For the herd...?

"Yeah! You know, for our race as a whole."

"You mean, for humanity?"

"Yes. For humanity. For mankind. What the fuck are we contributing to our herd?"

My mind raced furiously, searching for the answer I thought he wanted to hear. I came up with a mere title. "we, uh, we are commodities brokers." I cringed as he flipped his eyes towards the ceiling, exasperated. "Look..." I stammered, trying to hold his attention. "What we do is very important! If we punched out for good, just packed up our desks and got off the floor of the exchange, the entire flow of our culture would come to a grinding halt."

He sneered like he was enjoying some private cynical joke, or I had just said something incredibly naive. "Would it now?"

But now my pride had kicked in. "You bet your ass it would! If it weren't for us, there would be no way for Joe American to get his coffee from the Colombians, his rubber from the Africans, hell, without us, he can't even get his oil from the Arabs!"

"No?" He was still grinning viciously.

"No way!"

"Our ol' buddy Joe couldn't just travel to Colombia himself and buy his own coffee...?"

"Not and still keep his normal job."

"...or maybe just do without?"

I dropped my face into my hand, massaging my eyes with a thumb and forefinger. "Jesus Christ, Frank, you know all this! Hell! You're one of the best!" He winced. "You taught half the office everything they know." Remembering all of Frank's sales records and awards only made it harder to believe that this quivering wretch before me was the same man that mere days ago had been one of the cornerstones of our firm. The last of the pity was consumed by the growing revulsion at the comparison. "Frank, If you aren't happy with what you're doing any more, you can just quit." I snapped, trying to sound threatening.

Finally, he lost the grin, but it didn't seem to be out of fear for his job. "God," he murdered, "I only wish it was that easy. But I think it's already too late."

"Too late? What do you mean."

He looked off into space. "Our culture has gotten fat, Steve." He sighed. "Fat, lazy and slow. How much of the work done in our country is really necessary?" I started to respond, but he held up his hand. "I think things are changing. The world is going wild again." He shrugged. "Maybe it's for the best. They keep the herd healthy, you know. Weed out the bad genes."

With exaggerated effort, he hoisted himself from my chair. An odd feeling of resignation had fallen about him, a look of giving up blended with terror and loathing. He started towards the door.

"I really didn't expect you to understand." he muttered, tensing at the door, talking more to himself than to me. "Maybe it's for the best."

"Frank," I said softly, putting a hand on his shoulder. He flinched slightly. "You're tired. Why don't you go home, get some sleep. We can talk more about this over lunch tomorrow." I mentally slapped myself. The last thing I wanted was to be seen with a co-worker who was going down in flames.

"Yeah, sleep." he muttered. "It's been days. I am so tired of running."

He braced himself as I opened the door as if expecting a shock. There was nothing outside but the dark and the chirping crickets. He paused on the porch, turned around and looked back. For a moment, the old co-worker whom I knew from the office smiled back at me. I suddenly knew just how forced every smile I'd ever seen on his face had been. I reflexively forced the same passing-in-the-hallway smile. I held out my hand to shake. He didn't even see it.

"I wonder," he said plainly, "just how many of us have fallen so far behind." Then he turned slowly and shuffled off down the street. I watched him until I felt sure he wasn't going to come back, then I closed and locked the door.

* * *

I picked up my usual paper on my way into the office the next day. It sat on my desk all morning, and I wasn't aware until I read it at lunch that the picture on the front page was Frank Collins. He had been jumped by muggers in the park. He'd been killed - probably by a blow with a blunt object - then left for the stray dogs known to run wild in the park. They had eaten so much of his face that they had to identify the body by dental records. The weirdest part was that they'd left his wallet in his pocket, the $78 dollars inside it undisturbed. Probably some young, inexperienced punks who got in over their heads then panicked when things got wet. Considering the condition he was in when he left my house, it's no surprise he wandered into trouble.

That's what I told the police when they came to the office to talk to me about it. It's also what I tell myself as I lie in bed tonight listening to the neighbor's dogs howling at the moon.

Ten

Souvenirs

Things were finally beginning to turn around for Laura and me. After years of living the spartan life that seemed to be the price of being artists; cold studio apartments, pounding pavement in search of work, ramen boiling too long on an electric hot plate, and continually telling ourselves 'hold it together just a while longer then we're really gonna make it you'll see', it was really starting to happen.

Laura had been writing and playing her folk songs since long before we met. They were characterized by an elusive poignant fragility, much as she was. Imagine, as one of her earlier pieces bade you do, a woman born with no skin, just exposed nerves lying on raw flesh. She lives in a world of razor blades and broken glass and rusty nails. She could turn away and hide, but she embraces the world and swallows the screams 'cause the pain is just the price to be paid for living. Yes, melodramatic as all hell coming from me, but when she sang it, weaving her angelic soprano voice around the harp-like arpeggios she plucked from her acoustic guitar, you never doubted it for a second.

I was no stranger to broken glass either, only I hot-glued it to a stretched canvas with other broken shards of society's discards then splashed it with color until (I hope) it screamed at you to look and grabbed you by the lapels and shook you until you understood the anger or the joy or the irony or the sorrow or whatever other demon kept me from sleeping nights like normal folks.

Like so many other New York City boho-types, we haunted the coffee shops, sharing our work with other artists, lamenting over lattes the world's inability to perceive truly brilliant visionaries like ourselves. Then we'd go back to our little hovels and agonize over the current project, pulling our hair out and crying and wondering if we really were any better than all the hack artists writing and singing TV jingles or doing surf-and-turf oils that go oh-so-well over the sofa and if they don't then bring me a swatch of the fabric and I'll see to it that it does. We'd bask in those momentary epiphanies that crowned each newly finished piece, obsess over it for a moment, then throw on top of the heap of previously finished pieces and the whole fucking cycle started over again. We screamed our hearts and souls out into the void and waited for the echo.

It never came.

Until that winter.

Imagine our genuine surprise when Laura's songs started getting airplay on the college radio station. And soon thereafter I was picked up by a major gallery on 5th Street. Overnight, our world changed. There was a brief period of congratulations from our coffee house friends that *mostly* concealed their concern for our emotional well-being when we discovered it wouldn't last. When it *did* continue to last, the friends weren't so warm anymore, and without anyone speaking a single uncool word, we were forced into exile from the eternal twilight of the tragically hip.

Luckily, the gallery came complete with a built-in artist's ghetto of its own. Most of the close-knit (if not incestuous) stable of artists were enjoying some degree of success, and they welcomed Laura and me with open arms. Before long we felt right at home.

And what a home it was: a huge, warehouse-sized affair, with few external windows. All the studios were built around the outside walls of the nearly square floor plan. A hallway ran around the inside edge of these rooms, open to the huge vault-like atrium in the middle of the building. Each of us were assigned a stretch of wall close to our individual studios where we could display whatever we felt like putting out there for the world to see. If you climbed the stairs, or braved the rickety "fashionably retro" 1930's elevator, you could find the newest works that each of us were producing. Such displays occasionally generated sales, but more often served as a place to garner feedback for refinement before works could find their way downstairs to the gallery, where the real money was.

The ground floor was dominated by a sunken conversation pit. A few good sized trees grew out of pots near the corners, giving an outdoor feel to the place, especially in the early afternoon when the sun was beaming down from the huge skylight four floors above. The walls around this courtyard were where Mrs. Orowitz, the gallery's owner, hung the hottest pieces, which she hand picked herself. You could tell who was really being eaten up by the public by who dominated the ground floor.

Perhaps it was fear of performing in front of a whole new caliber of audience, but I found myself unable to muster my muse. I would sit in my studio at night, staring blankly at the canvas which stared right back at me, just as empty as it had been for the past three weeks. I left my studio door open so I could hear Laura playing her guitar in the courtyard below, her crystalline voice drifting like a wraith in the cavernous atrium. I would sit there, lower lip pinched between my fingers, not even really trying to see anything in that vast field of white that all but filled my field of vision, listening to the emptiness and loneliness echoing in her voice. My blood chilled, as somehow I knew, goddamn it I *knew*, that something vital inside her was drifting up to the skylight with her music and evaporating in the dim pink sodium vapor glow filtering in through the dusty glass.

I shook it off, chalking it up to too much espresso and not enough sleep, and began painting, hoping that the picture would happen without me. Actually it did, and though it was never one of my favorites, it got raves in all the must-be-seen-in art rags and commanded a personal record price from an "investment collector" from California. I would like to say that I was happy, but I was mostly worried about Laura. She'd been growing quiet.

At first, no one really thought much of it. She never was very loud to begin with. I think I'd heard her shout twice in the whole time we were together, and one of those was to get a cab. But she was talking less, even for her, and had developed a far-away look in her eyes, the corners of her mouth turned down. When someone would ask her if she was all right, she'd shrug it off and smile quietly and mutter something about playing with a new song idea. The new song, of course, never came, and the far-away look became more and more familiar.

Call me an idiot, but the first time I really began to get seriously worried was when I noticed that the gang was encouraging her to play more often than pure enjoyment would dictate. She always deferred, saying that she "wasn't in the mood right now" and fall back into her silence. I realized that it had been several weeks since I'd heard her sing anywhere but from the radio speakers.

By then, it was too late. Within days she wouldn't even respond to direct questions, merely following you around with her eyes. By week's end, her eyes quit following.

The doctors could find absolutely nothing wrong with her, nor could the psychiatrists provide any theories. She was a perfectly healthy, normal twenty-seven year old catatonic woman.

Once again, I found myself sitting and staring for hours at a blank canvas, only this one once held the spirit of the woman I loved. Months passed, timeless blurs of sorrow and pity and anger and hatred and jealousy and confusion. The collective was supportive, helping me to feed and clean her, making sure that I fed myself. Mrs. Orowitz was very understanding and kind, and didn't kick us out on our asses even though I hadn't produced so much as a postcard in eons. Eventually, I started coming to terms with the fact that I'd lost her, and unless I was prepared for some drastic measures, life was going to go on whether or not I was happy about it. I hauled my carcass into the shower for a long hot soak, a shave, and a cry. I emerged with a cruel sardonic thought jabbing me in my soul's bruises;

Hey kid, at least now you've got the perfect model for figure studies.

I briefly reconsidered suicide, then gave in to the black humor and laughed until my sides hurt. When the laughter finally spent itself, I wiped the tears from my eyes and took out my paints.

It felt good to be productive again. Often I had worried, usually through an alcohol saturated haze, if I would ever be able to paint again, but I was just putting the finishing touches on the third piece since Laura had "gone quiet". They were good work too! I had salvaged my status as a dynamic young talent, and my hopes for the future began to return. My spirits were high when a knock came at my studio door. It was Stephan, one of the older artists.

"Uh, David, You'd better come quick. It's *Laura.*"

My heart leapt with joy for a single beat, then froze in terror as the look on his ashen face said that it wasn't good. I dropped my brushes and rushed past him.

I don't remember what ran through my mind exactly, visions of seizures perhaps, or of her flopped over dead on the kitchen table. Whatever it was vanished as I reached the bottom of the stairwell and rushed out into the hall. Several of the women who had been caring for Laura were in the corridor, eyes wide with disbelief. They glanced up at me as I arrived, then slowly turned back to what Laura had become.

She was in front of the doors that led to the kitchen. There was no question that it was her face, still wearing that blank expression, open but unseeing eyes trained on some ambiguous spot just *over there* somewhere. But that face stared out from a flat, five-foot square of transparent blue glow the color of electricity, standing on edge oblivious to the laws of gravity. Her face was made of the same blue phosphorescence, bulging from the frame, filling the square like some huge Easter Island monolith staring off to sea. Through the blue neon fog of her face I could see into the kitchen behind her, and the utter confusion on the face of someone (I couldn't quite make out who) peeking around the door he or she was cowering behind.

Too stunned to be afraid, my mind desperately trying to grapple with what I was seeing, I staggered slowly, drunkenly towards her. There was no recognition in her eyes as I approached, no sign of life or sentience at all. She had become an artifact, a sculpture in pure energy and light without substance or mass, and the glow was slowly but perceptibly fading.

"Wait..." I muttered, barely audible, then built it into a scream. "WAIT!" I hurled myself in front of her, on my knees, hands clasped in white-knuckled fists, tears streaming down my face. I never once begged that it not really be happening – it was far too real to question– but merely prayed that she could still hear me and vomited my plea in a single consonant-anemic stream.

"Laura, I don't understand what's happening, I don't know what's happening to you! Please don't go, or if you have to go – wherever it is – please, at least take me with you! I love you! I'll be lost if you leave me like this..."

I couldn't force out any more coherent speech, dissolving into banshee moans and sobbing. I collapsed prostrate in front of this glowing mask like a crazed zealot before his idol. Warmth surrounded me, embraced me, removed me...

I was *inside* her. She *had* heard me, and somehow, reached out and absorbed me. Now I too was blue glow, and the blue glow was all that there was. She was all around me, yet I was also separate, like something gaseous, slowly dissipating, mixing, becoming one. There was stillness here, utter silence, and no perception of the material world which I had been sifted out of. I felt as though I was expanding, becoming more diffuse, she and I becoming *we*. I reached out to her, listening for her. Though she was much larger than I was, completely engulfing and surrounding me, I began to get the impression that I had become an integral part of her, and that perhaps our wills were now intertwined.

Flesh, I thought, forming the image in my mind as clearly as I could. I remembered stroking her silken skin and the feeling of sunshine browning my body on a summer afternoon. The feeling of a hot shower followed by cool clean sheets, of our bodies writhing in passion, made slick with sweat. *Wouldn't it be wonderful if we were flesh again?*

Vertigo seized me, a sudden falling and rushing forth as if being born or passed like excrement and I found myself lying on the grimy floor in front of her, soaked in sweat, shivering and defeated. I looked up at the huge mask, now a barely glowing steel gray and firmly opaque, and collapsed under the weight of such rejection into unconsoling unconsciousness.

Days passed before I was coherent enough to walk or speak normally. The gallery was closed. Some of the resident artists left and were never seen or heard from again, but most stayed, huddling together for strength and to endure the shock of something that defied any possible definition of reality we had walked on with such confidence before. The mask remained in the hall to prove over and over again that this wasn't just a serious drug trip or a strange dream that we would soon wake from with a start and a gasp.

The Face, as we all began to call what remained from Laura's transformation, had hardened into a hollow mask of vaguely pale-flesh colored material like hard vinyl, retaining her likeness in the same lifeless yet uncannily accurate way that a plaster casting does, then curving gracefully out into a flat plane, ending in a perfectly square boundary which we eventually measured to be 57 and one half inches on a side. (I would ponder the significance of the size and proportions for hours at a time, but to no avail.) The rubbery material was nearly a quarter inch thick, and reminded me of a doll I had had as a very small child. It was a stuffed fabric clown, with a molded vinyl face which was pouty and crying, a molded tear rolling down its molded cheek. I felt so bad for the eternally crying clown that I took a razor blade from my parent's medicine cabinet and very carefully shaved off the tear. What I hadn't counted on was the thinness of the material, and that the contours of the backside would match those of the front. I was left with a tear shaped hole in the poor clown's face, but he was no longer crying. Laura wasn't crying either. Later, in a grief-stricken attempt at irony, I pulled out a tube of blue acrylic and painted a corresponding tear on her cheek.

Eventually, the initial shock began to wear off, and the pragmatics of everyday life began to reassert themselves, as they always will after even the most traumatic events.

A question arose: "What are we going to *do* with her?" The general consensus was that since she no longer needed to be cared for, she was entirely my concern. Many were mortified to the point of hysterics, however, when I did what I thought seemed the only fitting and logical thing to do, considering.

I framed her and hung her in my section of the gallery.

I'd made her, hadn't I?

My wall was the south end of the second floor. I had a dozen odd pieces up, mostly throw-aways that I had been hoping someone who couldn't afford any of my ground floor paintings might settle for. I hung Laura on the right side. After twenty minutes of staring silently, I took down everything else.

In the months that followed, I spent very little time in my studio. I spent very little time at home. I began to haunt my wall like a tormented spirit unable to depart the place of its violent death. It no longer served as a mere passage from one side of the floor to the other, it was sacrosanct, a *temple*, and worship of the holy mask was around the clock.

I began to surround the face with objects. At first, they were just a few items that had belonged to Laura, left in my studio by default. A hairbrush. Her leather jacket. Some cassette tapes. I brought them out and placed them before the face like an offering. There they sat, unaccepted and inert, their presence unacknowledged.

Soon, I was bringing in other things from our apartment, starting with her guitar. Eventually, everything that was notably hers was piled in the hallway, arranged according to some cryptic geometry which I felt more than understood. Lines of identification cards, subway tokens, postcards and photos radiated outward, punctuated with larger items like a small wooden rocking chair she'd had since childhood, stuffed animals, favorite dolls, all marking intersections in the field. Each piece was a memento of the best times of her life, and a promise of rekindling that life anew.

It became impossible for anyone other than me to traverse the hall without disturbing something, and I, usually slathering drunk, horribly dirty and unshaved, stood guard to make certain that nothing was moved from its place.

Needless to say, my "installation" was, well, *noticed.* The gallery's regular crowd had heard something of the situation, usually vague, evasive references to my having "lost someone", others rather nervous lies about my wife's death. I was the poor, mad, artistic genius, delirious with grief, and expressing it through some obscure, arcane rite. Rather than repulse, this instead titillated the public greatly, and they would creep quietly upstairs to gaze at the complex labyrinth of icons, all pointing towards the impassive, unsettling likeness of the woman in question. They'd look for the meaning in the patterns, wondering if they weren't getting a privileged glimpse of the madness of a genius that might be discussed for decades to follow. Once, someone asked me if the new piece had a title. I laughed cynically and told him it was called *Souvenirs*.

There could be no question of her presence. Just looking at the hall one could *feel* her. Some said that I had infused the hall with my impressions of her, and complemented my ability at being able to convey them so tangibly. I denied such praise. It wasn't me. It was *her*.

Some nights, in a drunken rage, I would stand in front of her screaming, my voice echoing through the building. The others knew better than to approach me in the midst of such a fugue. Instead, they would just close their doors, grit their teeth, and say very little to me the following hung-over day. On one such night, as I flailed the unblinking face with accusations and curses, the chair *moved* – just a tiny little jerk, screeching audibly on the tile floor. I had only seen it peripherally, but there was no question of it. I fell silent and waited, but nothing else moved, there was no sound save the distant ticking of the clock downstairs in the kitchen. I stood there motionless for a while, then slowly took another swig from the bottle of vodka, wiped my chin, then stared for a while longer. It didn't move again.

During the day, I was able to maintain some kind of normality, but it was becoming evident that my welcome at the gallery was growing threadbare. Whatever kinship I had shared with these people was lost, almost certainly forever. They were actually surprised when I showed up - clean shaven, sober and properly dressed - for the open house social on the anniversary of the gallery's opening. The elite of the art world were there in their finest threads, sipping champagne. The best caterers were hired, the invites were exclusive, and empires could be founded on a tactful conversation. I hadn't been noted for my social graces lately, so it was no surprise they were reluctant to talk to me. It was odd to see the looks of trepidation on the faces of a group as I would approach, then watch the tension mostly melt away as I began conversing with a smile. Talk never drifted around to my work, though. The novelty of my mad display had worn off, the once intricate geometric organizations of my "installation" had entropied into heaps of trash, like some homeless person's back alley nest. Still, as long as I was clean and behaved myself, they were only too happy to discuss the weather or the spinach dip or Warhol's legacy with me.

It felt damned good to be back among the living. Between the companionship and the champagne, I had a heady feeling of belonging. We bid the last guests goodbye, followed shortly by Mrs. Orowitz, who clearly felt the night had been a smashing success. Although she refused to do business during the party, I felt certain that a she and a few key buyers would be back in the morning. We locked the door behind her, then retreated into the courtyard.

Spirits were still high, and the party continued into the evening, falling into the comfortable mellow groove found only amongst family or good friends. I wandered a bit, still basking in the forgotten glow of interaction, and somehow spun off from a conversation, wandered upstairs and found myself standing in front of her.

The goodwill and camaraderie dissolved instantly. For the first time, I saw the pathetic spectacle as everyone else must. Here was an altar to a lost loved one taken to degenerate extreme, grief corrupted into obsession bordering on necrophilia. The once mournful tribute had decayed into self-loathing and desperation. Bile surged in my throat as I became instantly aware of how I had chained myself to this, this, *thing*.

Rage flooded me, and I threw my empty glass at her. It merely rebounded off and shattered on the tile. Infuriated, I hurled myself at the face and began pounding and clawing at the rubber-like skin. The more I was unable to leave so much as a mark, the more crazed I became. Soon, I was completely out of control, and bit down on the left cheek. I managed to tear a chunk out with my teeth, leaving a ragged hole. Once I had a grip, I began tearing at the edges of the hole, shredding the face with both hands, biting and scratching and tearing, screaming and howling through clenched teeth. My nails were bleeding as I thrashed about, taking off dinner plate-sized chunks of mock flesh and hurling them behind me.

Suddenly, a doll hurled itself off the floor and smacked me in the back of the head. I whirled around to see it land on the floor, but no one was there. I sardonic smile twisted my face. So *now* she wanted to fight, eh? A bit late for that. My fury renewed, I grabbed the doll, tore it to pieces with my teeth, then lashed out at the face again.

A harmonica struck me in the back. A storm of cassette tapes followed, then a maelstrom of toys and other mementos rose up to assail me. I was bruised, perhaps even bleeding, but each impact just made me angrier. The little wooden rocking chair smacked against me, knocking me off my feet. I screamed and smashed the chair against the floor over and over until it was a scattering of splinters, regained my footing and tore at the face further. I was laughing then, imagining us entwined in some cruel apache dance, me ripping at her face, her pounding me with the remnants of the life she had abandoned.

When it was done, I sat panting on the floor with my legs splayed out in front of me, drenched with sweat and blood, dazed and exhausted. The hall was covered with a mulch of broken objects and shredded rubber. The frame still hung on the wall, a ragged fringe clinging to the wood where the face had been. I stared at the newly exposed patch of white wall, watching it brighten gradually as more and more sunlight began to filter in through the skylight. Footsteps padded up the stairs behind me, stopped at a distance, then came slowly closer, stopping again.

"Wow." It was Steve, one of the newer artists. "Made quite a mess up here."

I barked a laugh, turning slowly around. He was smiling timidly, his eyes showing more understanding than I would have thought possible. With expressions alone, we shared the same thought, the same mental sigh. *It's over.* I laughed again, watching his smile broaden to show his crooked teeth.

"You *are* gonna help me clean this up, aren't you?" He gestured towards the hall with his head, and held out his hand to help me up. I wiped the tears from my eyes and let him pull me to my feet. "I think we need some bags," he muttered. "I'll be right back."

He returned in moments, handing me a paper grocery sack. Slowly, numbly, I started scooping up the trash and filling the bag, not even looking at what I was throwing away. It didn't matter anymore. Handful by handful, we cleared the floor but it was apparent that a good sweeping was still needed. I mentioned this to Steve, and he trotted of to get the broom.

As I sat there waiting, a thin strumming drifted up from below, the delicate sound of a guitar being played. I didn't pay much attention at first, then my mind assembled the notes all at once, and my blood froze. It was one of *her* songs.

I dashed to the railing, my heart pounding in my ears. Below, in the conversation pit sat three of the resident artists, one with an old guitar in his lap. He noticed the look of shock in his companions, following their stares up to find me. My face must have been ghastly, for he paled, actually dropping the guitar.

I, I, I'm sorry, man, I wasn't, I mean, I didn't think that..." he stammered, panic stricken.

"No, no. It's okay." I muttered, laughing at myself and shaking my head. "I mean it. It's all right. I just thought..." I trailed off, it was too much to say aloud. I'd dared to hope...

The hair on the back of my neck stood up. I felt someone behind me, as if they had snuck up on me, but I knew that no one had. I turned slowly around.

It was Laura. She sat on her legs awkwardly, unsteadily like a newborn calf. Her eyes were filled with fear and confusion, darting around the hall, then stopping on me. She worked her mouth as if she wanted to speak, but didn't know how.

A motion in my peripheral vision startled me. I was reluctant to look away, afraid she might disappear if I took my eyes off of her. No, if it was a hallucination, it was best to release it there and then.

Steve had returned, standing dumbly in the hallway, staring alternately at me then at her. I smiled at him, nodding. Yes, he saw her too, and she was still there when I looked back. Her eyes were pleading, wanting. I took a step towards her, tears streaming down my face. Slowly, she turned towards the wall, looking up at the ragged frame hanging on the wall, then looked back to me for an explanation. I had none to offer.

Gently, I took her into my arms. She tensed for a moment, as if afraid I'd hurt her, then relaxed and threw her arms around me, pulling on me tightly and burying her head in my shoulder. Our bodies shuddered with joyful sobbing, clinging to each other, afraid that we might become separated again if we let go.

Others were slowly coming up now, approaching with trepidation and awe. Some were crying, others merely stared.

I held her away from me for a moment so that I could see her, verify once more that it was *really* her. She smiled, her face torn between joy and frustration with being unable to speak. I kissed her, her lips, her eyes, her whole face, then pulled her into another deep embrace.

"It's okay," I whispered in her ear. "There's no hurry, no need to rush. You're back now, and that's all that's important."

She pulled me closer, soaking my shirt with tears, and I knew she was smiling.

Eleven
Whispers and Frost

My battered Datsun stood out from the line of Mercedes, Lexuses and Beemers like a missing tooth. The oxidized orange car was exactly what you think of when you try to picture a typical college student's ride. But then, California Institute of the Arts was no typical college.

The fact that I was accepted to CalArts was something of a fluke. I didn't really think they'd buy my pathetic attempt to sell the piss-poor production values of the short video I'd submitted as deliberate and ironically *retro*, kind of like the Pixelvision 2000 fad that sprung up in the early 90's. But not only did I get in, they awarded me a sizable scholarship.

Good thing too. There was no way in hell I'd have been able to cough up the completely insane amount of money they were getting per semester. It was the price one paid to be at a school that focused entirely on creativity and experimentation rather than on academics. It also explained the big ticket cars parked in rows outside the Film Arts building.

I slammed the filthy hatchback and started slinging gear bags over my shoulders and around my neck. This was the true mark of a CalArts freshman, carrying your own gear. The school was set up not unlike a Hollywood movie studio, with a very clear pecking order and no illusions precisely where one fit into it. Seniors ruled the roost, with their own feature projects, and preferential treatment at the equipment cage. Juniors filled the skilled positions on the senior projects, running camera, setting up lights, and dreaming of when they'd be able to direct next year. Sophomores were the raw manpower, pulling cables, securing locations, and the like. We lowly freshmen were the pack mules, forever hauling crates and bags from place to place, grumbling about the money we were spending and wondering when we'd actuallyget to start working on films in any kind of meaningful way.

None of which meant that we weren't also expected to be shooting. At least once a week we were supposed to shoot, edit and show short bits theoretically designed to explore some aspect of cinema, but I wasn't seeing the point of most of this "homework." To supposedly get a better grasp of the interplay between light and shadow, one of the professors set up an army surplus 12 man tent in one of the smaller studios, put a cluster of can lights in its center pointed outward toward the walls, and then brought in a gaggle of dancers from the Interpretive Dance program and had them cavort around inside the tent. Our assignment was to shoot the tent from the outside, capturing the overlapping multi-colored shadows being cast on the tent walls and cut it to a piece of music.

It just didn't make any sense to me. It seemed that if there was anything to be learned from the exercise, it was in setting up the lights, learning where to place them so that the shadows would make the most interesting patterns, but that part had already been done for us. But this didn't stop the other students from shooting like they were creating porn, swooping in until the lens almost touched the canvas and then flying back out with as much camera swim as possible.

The TA accepted the VHS tape I'd handed him as if it were dripping with piss. The masquerade that I was using inexpensive low-tech as a matter of style didn't fly with most, especially when it meant that they had to lug an ancient, heavy VCR into the class once a week for just one student. Most of the other students either turned in a DVD or merely plugged their tricked out laptops directly into the projector.

I slunk back to my seat, feeling the TA's scorn on the back of my neck. Few looked up as I passed. It was clear to most that I just didn't belong here, that somehow one of the unwashed masses had scaled the wall into their exclusive little playground.

That indictment seemed to be confirmed when the professor called out my name and the old VCR spun up in the back of the room with an audible whine, prompting chuckling from some of the other students. On the screen in the front of the room, my piece faded in, and to the thumping hiss of Nine Inch Nails' "Closer", I did my best impression of an epileptic cameraman. The piece lasted the requisite three minutes – and I mean *to the second* – and then faded to black.

Professor Galliard stood up from his desk, shaking his head. "Mister Afton, I see your sticking to your stylistic guns," he began dolefully. I shrunk in my seat even further. "But even in the analog dark ages, our ancestors understood the dangers of video clipping. This whole exercise was all about maximizing the exposure range of your image, keeping your darks dark without losing detail, keeping your brights bright without blowing out. Your footage looks like you processed it through a photocopier. Did you even bother to calibrate your field monitor?"

Unlike most of his questions, Galliard expected a reply this time. "I… I didn't have a field monitor."

"I thought as much." Disappointment dripped from his voice. "I believe we've discussed this several times before. The viewfinders of most cameras are notoriously inaccurate. I'm guessing you used a camera with a black and white eye piece, which is barely clear enough for framing, much less getting a decent reading on your video levels. If you hope to pass this class, I strongly suggest that you make a point of using a properly calibrated field monitor on your next assignment."

And with no further comment, the next student's piece began to roll in all its crystalline digital glory.

* * *

"Dude, that was harsh." Steven Campbell, one of the few decent rich kids caught up to me in the hall. "I thought he was going to kill you."

"I wish he had. Where the fuck am I supposed to get a field monitor? The seniors have all the gear from the equipment cage."

"You're using all analog gear, right? Why don't you go poke around in the pit?"

"The what now?"

"*The pit.* There's a junk room down in the basement where they keep all the old shit that no one wants to use anymore."

"Oh great, that's *exactly* what I need, some piece of shit monitor carved out of wood."

Campbell shrugged. "Hey man, beggars can't be whiners. Wood or not, you better get some kind of monitor before next week or start thinking about a career in fast food. Speaking of which, I'm going to In and Out. You want to come with?"

"You buying?"

Campbell scowled, but tilted his head towards the parking lot.

* * *

"Hello?"

I stood at the top of the stairs to the basement, but it was so dark down there that I couldn't see the bottom. I started down, one hand firmly on the handrail.

By the time I reached the floor, my eyes had adjusted from the blinding Southern California sunshine, and I could see that it wasn't as dark as I'd thought. The "basement" didn't look much different from the other mazes of corridors at CalArts, except that this one was narrow, lit by yellowing fluorescents and far less clean. Here and there large boxes were stacked against the graffiti textured walls, carts and hand trucks were abandoned in lonely corners. The air conditioning hummed audibly in the silence as I walked slowly down the hallway, squinting at each door for some kind of markings that simply weren't there. I tried a couple of knobs, but each was securely locked.

I began to wonder if Campbell hadn't sent me on some kind of freshman hazing, tricking me into searching forever for some mythical treasure trove of free gear. I was just about to give up when a sharp tapping sound startled me. I whirled around to find a woman in her mid thirties walking toward me, her high heels clicking loudly on the tile floor.

"You look lost," she stated plainly as she got close. "Can I help you?"

"I hope this doesn't sound stupid, but I'm looking for some kind of junk room full of old video equipment."

"Oh, *the pit*." She beckoned for me to follow her.

She led me around a corner, opened a non-descript door and reached in to turn on the lights. I peered past her into a small storeroom packed unceremoniously from floor to ceiling with televisions, old VCRs, video switchers, and countless rack mount components that I could only guess what they were.

The woman started to walk away, but I stopped her with a raised finger. "If I find something I'd like to use, where do I sign it out?"

She laughed. "Just help yourself. As long as you bring it back when you are done, you can use any of this stuff."

"Want me to lock the door when I'm done?"

"Nah, no one ever locks this door. Who would steal this crap?" And with that, she left me alone with the electronic past.

I stepped slowly into the room. The place was like a museum of discarded equipment, most of which seemed to date back to the late seventies or early eighties. Some of it was disassembled, probably cannibalized for parts. A couple of the television monitors had smashed in screens, and I could only imagine mortified students returning from a shoot that had gone south to return their broken gear.

I was thrilled. How many others knew this place was here? Clearly none of the proto-Spielbergs would lower themselves enough to use *any* analog gear, much less stuff as old, battered and positively déclassé as this stuff.

Since the first order of business was finding a field monitor, I poked around for a small-ish TV that might do the job. I ruled out any that were too big to fit in the back of my car, or that I couldn't lift and carry by myself. I finally spotted an old studio monitor from the early '80s that looked perfect for my purposes and wriggled it loose from the crowded shelf it languished on. There was a sort of workbench against the far wall, so I hauled it over and plugged it in to test it. It crackled loudly when I poked the power switch. After a moment, the image faded up, and displayed a thick texture of twenty years worth of burned-in text.

"Fuck," I spat, returned the useless monitor to the pile, and resumed the hunt.

* * *

"Hey Afton, where did you dig up the antique?"

I glanced up from the camera to find a cluster of snobs laughing at the monitor I had balanced precariously on a wobbly thrift store microwave cart.

"Don't knock it," I sneered back, feigning superiority. "No matter how much you guys pay for LCD screens, they can't touch the sheer luminosity range you get with *glass*."

"Jesus, how much does it weigh? Is that table rated for it?"

"How is your grandmother supposed to watch her stories while you've got her TV?" Apparently none of them thought they could top that, so they just drifted away laughing hysterically.

My motivation collapsed. Once again I started wondering if I really had what it took to work in the movie biz. Slowly, I unscrewed the camera from the tripod and started breaking down. I tossed most of gear into the back of my car, but I was damned if I was going to take the two-ton monster to my tiny studio apartment and haul it up the steps. I set the car alarm and started wheeling the cart back to the pit.

* * *

The fluorescent lights flickered and hummed for a minute before they finally built up enough charge to ignite. I didn't feel like going to my next class, so I took it upon myself to see just how far back this collection of relics went. I knew that the school dated back to 1961, when Walt Disney provided the funding to create a breeding ground for the next generation of animators, but had only been at the Valencia campus since '71.

I excavated a TV with a round picture tube that looked to be from the late fifties. Curious to see if it still worked, I perched it on the workbench, plugged it in, then hesitated a moment before touching the huge plastic knob. I didn't think there was really any danger of it exploding, so I twisted it on.

A loud pop issued from the back of the set, the screen flashed like it took my picture, and a curl of acrid blue smoke writhed out from the vent slots in the case. I quickly yanked the plug from the outlet and stood back laughing until the potentially carcinogenic smoke cleared.

I entertained a moment of elation when I found a pair of pro grade VHS tape decks and a matching switcher/controller, but hearing the loose bits and pieces rattling around inside the decks when I picked them up shattered the dream.

"Well," I pondered, "if I can't have my own editing suite, maybe I can at least cobble together my own TV lounge."

There were a number of studio monitors like the one I was using in the field, but none of them were true *televisions,* as they had no built in tuner and couldn't receive anything being broadcast.

I lifted off yet another old character generator and revealed a knob straight out of an old science fiction movie serial. It was huge had elaborately fluted edges, and was surrounded by dial bearing multiple bands of arcane numbers. Thinking I may have found a new grand champion in the antiques derby, I started shifting the boxes it was buried under with renewed vigor. When I finally extricated it from the stack, I stood a moment trying to figure out what the hell I was looking at. It wasn't as old as I first thought, but it still had to be from the late fifties, maybe early sixties at the latest. It was heavier than it looked, and I had to strain to hump it up onto the workbench. I blew off the front, and like a genie billowing out of a bottle, the clouds of dust parted to reveal an etched metal tag that read:

WESTINGHOUSE 2800 TELEVISION RECIEVER/TRANSMITTER

I blinked at the arcane device. It was unlike any tuner I'd ever seen before. There were no channel numbers to click through, just raw frequency numbers like an old radio. If it still worked, this was the answer to getting a watchable TV going. Without investing too much hope, I connected my field monitor, made sure I wasn't touching anything metal and plugged it in. Nothing happened at first, so I decided to risk switching it on. I checked to make sure I had a clear lane to the door, and then flipped the power switch.

A light came on under the dial, but other than that and a slight humming sound, there was no reaction; no clouds of smoke, no frying electronics. After a moment, the monitor burst into snow, the speaker hissing loudly. I turned the sound down to a more bearable level, and slowly began turning that huge knob. Almost immediately, a hazy, wobbly picture formed, and through the hiss I could hear someone speaking in Spanish. It worked! I began searching for a station that came in better.

I was able to find several stations, but without an antenna, none of them came in clearly enough to watch. I dashed around until I found a snarl of speaker wire and tossed it up over one of the shelving units, then wrapped the exposed ends around the leads in back of the receiver. It helped slightly, but even with the makeshift antenna, I was too deep in the bowels of the building to get clear reception.

I tried one last round of the dial before giving up entirely. I muttered, "There's no way in hell I can talk the school into running cable down here..." but stopped as the TV squawked and a burst of color flashed on the screen. It was the strongest signal I'd found yet, and I finessed the dial to bring it in as clear as possible.

The screen erupted into swirling psychedelic patterns, and a slightly distorted man's voice was talking over it.

"...terrible snow that year except they had no coal and they froze to death in their cabin their bodies were discovered the following spring by some hunters who wandered through the area looking for the year's first bucks only they hadn't brought their guns or fishing gear either so they would have to eat their shoes which tasted like licorice but neither of them thought that was odd even though they didn't care for licorice much so they invited their friends on a picnic I really love a good picnic in spring especially a really nice mustard on homemade bread...."

At first I figured I was watching one of those new "what the fuck are they doing" commercials that were all the rage. I glanced at the dial to see what channel I was on, but I wasn't aware of any station that broadcast on that frequency.

After a minute or so, I continued scanning the dial, but as before, I couldn't find another signal that came in clear enough to watch. I shrugged and went back to the strong channel to see if the commercial or whatever it was had ended.

"...opiates smuggled in quarts of milk and hidden in a piñata and hurled into the sky where it exploded into a burst of shrapnel and rose petals that float lazily onto the surface of the lake causing ripples that expand outward growing in intensity until they become a tidal wave that wipes out a small coastal village in Taiwan but the disaster had been foretold in a dream where a lovely young girl on horseback rode out of the dark forest in search of a cobbler who could fix her crystal vase that had been knocked to the floor by her clumsy oaf of a brother...."

It had been at least ten minutes, but the voice was still droning on without end, the trippy colors continuing to ebb and flow on the screen. I realized that there was no way that anyone could ramble on and on like that without ever taking a breath, so it had to be cut together. But *why?* The only people who would put together something so meaningless and pretentious…

…and suddenly it dawned on me why the signal was so clear. It had to be coming *from inside the building.* This was yet another lame project by one of the countless Cal Arts students with far more money than ideas. I shook my head in disgust. The visuals were probably an off-the-shelf screen saver, and the narrator, while he had a nice soothing voice and professional delivery, was uttering total nonsense, just more drivel for the posers.

Glancing up at the clock I realized that I was late for my next class, *Concepts in Visual Communication.* "They'd love this crap", I muttered, and flicked the power switch off.

* * *

The rest of the day was just as useless. I took my requisite notes, sat through endless minutes of glossy but vapid footage, and sulked quietly in the back of the classes. When my last session was out, I retreated back to the pit to gather up my gear and go home. Before disconnecting the field monitor, something made me turn on the receiver again.

"… calendar was established in the 13th century by an obscure clerical order in the Basque mountains where they lived a tranquil existence of animal husbandry and grew wheat and barley in fields completely isolated from the war which had gown out of the region's growing dissatisfaction with the moral fiber of their leaders and the total disregard for how butterscotch pudding was underrated even though it was vastly superior to the more popular chocolate…"

I shook my head. Did they have this thing running around the clock? I wondered how long the piece was. Surely it would have to loop around again. I sat back and waited for any hint of repetition, watching the undulating patterns flare and fade on the screen. The hypnotic imagery was very relaxing, and I unfocused my eyes and relaxed, letting the nonsense words flow across my mind. Every now and then it would start to sound like it might actually mean something, but any trace of narrative thread melted away as quickly as it formed.

Before I realized it, I'd been soaking in the surreal project for over an hour.

And there still hadn't been a single repeated sentence.

OK, so maybe there *was* something interesting about it, if only it's sheer volume. I started to wonder if the voice was computer generated, as automatic and random as the picture. If so, it could go on like that forever, but if that was the case it was the most amazingly realistic synthesized voice I had ever heard.

And I realized that I was hooked. I had to find out who was behind the madness and talk to them.

* * *

The last stragglers filed out of the classroom, but I stayed behind to talk to Mr. Dorcer. He was an old school broadcasting guy from way back, probably taught classes with most of the gear down in the pit.

"Why Mr. Afton, you're usually one of the first to bolt for the door."

"Uh, yeah, I, I'm hoping you can help me with something."

He raised an eyebrow. "Shoot."

"I, uh, I'm trying to find a student, or maybe it's a group of students that's working on some kind of video thing here on campus."

Mr. Dorcer smiled wryly. "Could you be more specific?"

"Yeah, sorry, it's kind of a spoken word thing, complete gibberish narrated over abstract visuals, and it seems to go on and on endlessly."

"Sounds engrossing." His sarcasm was palpable.

"Uh, yeah, it doesn't sound like much, but there's something about it that's kinda, well, *fascinating* after a while.

"Well, it doesn't ring any bells. Where did you see it?"

"I watched it on TV. I'm pretty sure it's being broadcast from here on campus."

That opened his eyes. "Broadcast? You must be mistaken. Unless…"

"Unless?"

Mr. Dorcer looked around, then leaned in closer. "I ran a pirate TV station back when I was going to school here. I wonder if someone is keeping up the tradition."

I nodded. "Hmmm. It could be something like that… Is there some way to find out where it's coming from?"

He rubbed his chin. "You could always triangulate it. Rig a receiver with a directional antenna. Turn it until the signal comes in the strongest. Then draw a line on a map in that direction from your location. Then do it again in several spots, the farther apart, the better. The signal will be coming from the place where all the lines cross. That is, unless they are moving around to avoid being caught that way."

I nodded. "Yeah, that makes sense. All right, thanks."

Mr. Dorcer smiled. "See you next week." I was almost out the door when he shouted after me. "Oh, and Michael…" I stopped and turned around. "It's good to see you taking an interest in something class related. Maybe your interest in analog video isn't a cop-out after all."

* * *

"...only because the Jews owned controlling interest in most of the companies involved and none of the grommets prevented the fabric from ripping down Route 66 in a covered wagon filled with teeth that had known the bite of young flesh sliding across satin waves of grain growing in the golden sunlight beaming down like a benediction from above the stratosphere offering no trace of the onslaught lurking behind the armoire leaning in the corner and concealing the holes drilled in the wall and filled with marzipan except for the one that the neighbor was peering through..."

Even after two weeks, the voice had droned on without interruption or repetition, or even taking a breath. I had been asking around the entire time, and had even gone so far as to post a couple of notices on the campus bulletin board asking for any information about the transmission. If anyone knew anything about it, they were keeping it to themselves.

Despite Mr. Dorcer's disclaimer, I was still certain the signal was coming from on campus, or at least somewhere very nearby. I had hauled the receiver home and tried to tune the frequency in question from there, but got nothing but static for my trouble.

I let the program run in the background as if I were listening to the radio as I went back to sifting through the surplus gear. I had begun to tidy it all into piles of things that had the potential to be useful and stuff that was too far gone. I picked up fairly large audio board leaning in the corner that I decided should go in the latter category and uncovered an old desk microphone. Everything about it was familiar, from the plastic housing, it's silhouette, the old frayed cable and the arcane looking connector. I instantly knew that it went with the Westinghouse receiver. I set the audio board aside and picked up the mic.

The connector was dusty, but it went into the socket on back of the box perfectly. I'd totally forgotten that the unit was a transmitter as well.

A notion popped into my head; if I started broadcasting on the same frequency as the voice, would the people behind it even know? If I interfered with their transmission enough, might they come looking for me? It seemed like it might be a way to make contact with them. There was only one way to find out. I keyed the mic and said "Hey, jabbermouth, give it a rest."

The voice stopped, the swirling light show faltered a moment, and then went into overdrive. For a moment I wondered if it were possible that I'd crashed the computer that was running the program, but after a moment, the voice picked up again.

"…a voice in the darkness and I don't think that was me thinking it but it's so hard to tell could there really be someone out there or did I just imagine it I've been alone for so long and it's not the first time I've thought I heard something and it turned out to be nothing but my hopes and fears of day when Americans were no longer free to buy ice cream and walk down the street that led out of town and across a bridge that crosses a high gorge filled with mist from a majestic waterfall below…"

I keyed the mic again. "Can you hear me?"

"…I did hear it! Yes! I hear you! Are you real or am I making you up? Is this… Are you God?"

The voice was silent. I answered. "Dude, I don't know what you are smoking, but I want some."

"I don't understand. Who are you?"

"Who are you?"

"I am... I am... I have a name, but it's been so long...What a silly and pathetic thing to not be able to remember one's own name. It's not very clear now, I know it wasn't always like this... there was a before time when I could see and hear and smell and taste and there were others, so many others, I remember them, though some seem real and some can't possibly be. It's so hard to concentrate like this because lights twinkle in the sky over a field blanketed in freshly fallen snow broken only by a single trail of footsteps..."

I gaped at the monitor. The psychedelic light show was beginning to slow down to its slower, measured rhythm, and the voice had returned to babbling. There was no way this could be a computer program, at least I didn't think so. It had responded to me in real time, and seemed to understand what I was saying. I opened the channel and spoke again. "Hey, I want to know more about your project. It's interesting. Are you here at CalArts?"

"My project? There have been so many over the years, but that was a long time ago."

"I mean *this one*! The one you are doing right now! Where are you?"

"I don't understand. I don't know where I am. Am I not dead?"

"If you were dead, you wouldn't be talking to me. Seriously, man, what are you on?"

"I am not on anything. I am not anywhere. I am alone in the darkness talking to myself. If this is not death, and you are not an angel, then what are you?"

"Uh, I'm a college student. Film major. My name is Michael Afton.

"You are among the living?"

"Well, *duh*."

"How are you speaking to me? Are you a medium?"

"What? No! I'm using a really old television transmitter."

"Television? Then… I'm not dead, at least, not as I know death." The screen saver changed abruptly, and the tenor of the voice took on the unmistakable sound of sobbing. "Thank you, sweet merciful God."

"Whoa, take it easy there, fella! I don't know what your trip is but you are seriously creeping me out here."

"I apologize, it's just that I thought that it would be like this forever, that I was in Limbo, or perhaps even hell. But I thought that even Hell would have others in it. Yours is the first voice other than my own that I've heard in… I… I'm not sure how long. Longer than I can remember. I'm still not completely certain that I'm not imagining you to break the crushing loneliness."

I had to laugh. "You aren't imagining me. But that's OK, I'm not sure you aren't making this all up yourself."

"Why would I do such a horrible thing?"

"I don't know. Maybe to mess with me. Maybe some weird kind of performance art."

"Performance. Art. Yes, those words seem right. I was some kind of performer, or an artist once. It's all a haze now, I can't fathom it at all."

I shook my head. He sounded so sincere, so desperate. "Hey, you still haven't told me what to call you."

He was silent a moment. "There are many names darting around in my mind. The one that seems to stand out most clearly is Mickey."

"OK, Mickey, it is, like the mo…" I glanced up at the clock and boggled. "OH JESUS CHRIST! I'm late for class. Look, Mickey, I have to jet…"

"NO! Please don't leave me alone!! I don't know if I can take it…"

"Hey, chill! I'll be back later. If you are still on, we can talk some more."

"Please, don't go…"

I switched off the transmitter and scrambled out into the corridor.

* * *

It had been worse than I thought. Not only had I been late for class, but I'd totally spaced that we had a quiz to boot. The professor chewed me out in front of the class and said there would be no make-ups, I'd just have to take the point loss and try to make it up during the rest of the semester. Feeling completely defeated and humiliated, I retreated back to the relative safety of the pit.

I waited for the door to click closed behind me before switching on the receiver.

"…there was a voice that wasn't mine and I didn't make it up he said his name was Michael Afton and that he was a living college student talking to me via a television transmitter which makes no sense at all but I heard him I know I did! I know I did! I know I did…"

"Dude, have you been going on like that since I left?"

"You are back! I knew I didn't make you up! I'm not alone anymore!"

"Look, man, you can't blow a gasket because I sign off now and then. I can't be on the air twenty-four seven like you."

"I don't understand. What do you mean by 'on the air'?"

"Your program. I've been tuning in for weeks now. I'd like to know how you're doing it, and what it's for. Are you a student too?"

"I don't understand anything you are saying. My program? I used to have a television program. I'm fairly certain that's true. But that was a long time ago, when I was still alive, I think."

"Call it whatever you like. I'm talking about the words you've been saying, along with this trippy screen saver you're running."

"My words? You've been listening all along?"

"Like I said, just the last two weeks. How long have you been broadcasting?"

"I didn't know that I was. I've just been talking to myself, to keep myself company, to try and remember."

I scratched my head, trying to figure out if this guy was genuinely crazy, messing with me, or just staying in character. Ultimately, I figure it didn't matter. "So where are you?"

"I don't know. I can't see anything at all. It's dark here, very cold and very dark."

"But you weren't always there."

"I... I don't think so. I remember things, but it's been so long I can't picture them clearly."

"What's the last thing you remember?"

"I was sick. So much pain, for so long. Then the pain released. I thought I had died, but then I was here and have been here ever since."

If he was acting, he was good. His voice practically dripped with sincerity, and I found myself oddly moved.

"Where am I?"

"That's *my* question. You are one seriously messed up freak, and I want to party with you."

"A party? Is it my birthday?"

"Yeah, it's your birthday, and I've got a present for you. Where should I bring it?"

"I have no idea."

The act was getting old, and I was getting pissed. "Fine, be a dick about it. I'll find you the hard way." I switched off the receiver.

* * *

It took three weeks to find a company on the web that had the old style directional TV antenna and order one. When it finally arrive in the mail I pulled out the crumpled newspaper packing to unveil what looked like a miniature radar dish adorned with cute cartoon lightning bolts. While I had been waiting for it to arrive I'd been giving "Mickey" the cold shoulder. Every few days I'd tune in to see if he was still broadcasting, and he always was. Once, he'd just been screaming my name over and over. It creeped me right the fuck out. He eventually settled back into his random monologue, just as it was when I first picked it up.

Back in the pit, I loaded the receiver onto the cart, added the old reciever and the spiffy new antenna, and prayed that the cart wouldn't collapse under the weight. I had to "liberate" several extension cords from various classrooms, but I eventually set up my first station in the quad just outside the video building.

"Hey Afton, what the hell are you doing now?"

I looked up. "Hey Steve. I'm picking up signals from aliens. One of them says he's your dad."

He laughed. "Funny. No, really."

I beckoned him closer. "I'm looking for a pirate television station."

Campbell's eyes opened wide. "Seriously? Here on campus?"

I nodded. "Yeah. Here, I'll show you." I turned on the receiver, but got nothing but static. I double checked the frequency, and slowly rotated the antenna in a full circle. Still nothing."

"That's gripping."

"Shit. He must have stopped broadcasting."

Campbell laughed. "Well, good luck with the hunt. Don't get yourself probed."

* * *

Once I got back to the pit, I turned on the receiver, but still got nothing. I tried rotating the antenna, and nearly immediately, the old familiar light show bloomed across the tube, Mickey's mindless patter issuing from the speakers.

"There you are…" I muttered. I adjusted the antenna again, and found that I had to have it pointed straight at the back wall in order to pickup the signal. Turned a fraction of a degree to either side, the picture dissolved into static.

It had never occurred to me that the broadcast might be coming from down in the basement. It didn't make any sense. If you want to reach the biggest area possible, you put your transmitter as high as you could.

I quickly wheeled the cart out into the hall, playing out extension cords as I went. From just the other side of the door, I turned the antenna until I brought the program back into clarity. There was a marked difference to the angle now, nearly 45 degrees to the heading I had inside the room. I rolled the cart another ten feet down the hall, and took another reading. This time, the antenna pointed directly at the next door down the hall from the pit.

"No fucking way…" He was in the next goddamned room! No wonder I hadn't gotten anything upstairs. The signal was actually quite weak, and the only reason I'd found it at all was sheer proximity. I reached for the handle, but recoiled the instant I made contact.

It was cold.

It wasn't an ordinary door at all. It was thick, with heavy hinges, and secured with a heavy padlock. A filthy rubber gasket sealed it to the frame. It was plastered with so many stickers and flyers that it almost blended in with the graffiti choked wall, but didn't disguise the fact that for whatever reason, here in the basement under CalArts was a walk-in freezer.

It was so incongruous all by itself that I nearly forgot for a moment how I'd found it. From all indications, the pirate television station that I had been obsessed with for so long was being broadcast *from inside.*

I scoured the door for some clue what the freezer was for. There was a small sheet of paper tacked near the door handle that I'd mistake for a flyer, but was actually a maintenance log from a company called Santa Clarita Industrial Gasses. On the 15th of each month, someone had dated and initialed the sheet, indicating any work done. The most recent item on the list read "recharged liquid nitrogen."

A completely preposterous idea lodged in my mind, one so ridiculous that it didn't bear consideration. However, as unlikely as it was, *it made sense.*

I nearly jumped out of my skin when I heard footsteps coming from around the corner at the end of the hall. I lurched and scrambled the cart back into the pit before they could see me. I stood motionless with my back against the door until the footsteps passed by and receded into the distance. When I felt it was safe, I peeked out into the hall to make sure I was alone, then closed the door, and for the first time, locked it from the inside.

The receiver was still on, so I tuned in the signal.

"groves of macadamia trees swaying gently in the cool breeze provided a home to bird of every description except a flamingo wearing a straw boater danced about until it tripped over his cane and fell to the stage…"

I keyed the microphone. "Uh, hey."

"Hello! Is this Michael Afton? Have you come back to me?"

I winced. "Yeah, uh, sorry about being gone so long. I've been looking for you."

"Have you found me?"

"Yeah, I think I have. And if I'm right, I know who you are now."

"My name isn't Mickey?"

I smiled. "No, I believe… I'm pretty sure your name is Walt."

The psychedelic light show froze motionless for a single heartbeat, then flared into the brightest white the monitor could produce.

"Walt."

The colors returned, but this time the pattern was somehow sharper, more defined, and was fluctuating much more quickly.

"Yes. I remember now. My name is Walter."

The hairs on my arm were standing up as if electrically charged. The light show crystallized, and melted into a warped image of two small circles resting atop a larger one.

"Where am I? What happened to me?"

I swallowed hard. "I... You... I mean, this is so hard to believe. You could be totally yanking my chain, but God help me, I don't think you are..."

"I don't understand."

"You are frozen."

Walt was silent for a moment. *"Cryonics."*

"I guess so. I mean, I don't know what else you'd call it."

"Then I am dead."

"There have always been stories – jokes, really – urban legends that when you died, they had you frozen so they could bring you back someday, but the stories always say that you are hidden somewhere in Disneyland."

"Disneyland!" He sounded genuinely excited. *"My park! Tell me, Michael, is Disneyland still open?"*

I laughed. "Oh dude, you have no idea. You wouldn't even recognize it now. It's huge."

"They… they changed it?"

"Oh yeah. They bought up most of the land around the original park and built The California Adventure, closed some the cheesier rides for kids, and started reworking the big attractions with movie tie-ins wherever they could."

"What year is it now?"

"It's 2007."

"That… That can't be possible."

"Sorry man, I'm not jerking you around."

"I have been dead for forty years."

I wasn't sure what to say. I'd never spoken with a frozen corpse before.

"But they still remember me?"

"Are you kidding? You are a household name! Everyone in the world loves you!"

"Did they ever finish the park in Florida?"

I laughed again. "Florida, France *and* Japan"

"Astounding. And the studio? Do they still make movies?"

"Oh yeah, several a year, and they are always blockbusters. Although they mostly do CGI now instead of traditional animation."

"CGI?"

"It stands for Computer Generated Images. It just means that they make the movies on a computer instead of drawing them by hand."

"That sounds horrible. No machine could ever create art. True art can only come from the soul and hands of a man."

"Well, it's complicated. It's still done by artists, they just use the computer as a tool."

"Tell me, Michael, what is the world of tomorrow like? Is it full of wonders? Has science eased man's burden? Do we walk on other worlds?"

"Heh. I guess I do live in the future, at least as far as you're concerned. It's allright, I guess. It's not like you guys thought it was going to be, all Tomorrow Land and shit."

"Tomorrow Land was always my favorite. Is it still popular?"

"Uh, actually, it got pretty dated after a while, and they ripped it out."

"What?"

"Twice, actually. Now it's all *steampunk*, you know? Like Jules Verne. Victorian with rockets and ray guns."

"They changed Tomorrow Land. I can't believe it."

"They had to. After the moon landings, your vision of the future looked kinda, well, it was *too optimistic.*"

"I don't understand. We were almost to the moon when I... last I recall."

"Yeah, we landed on the moon. Brought back a bunch of rocks."

"Has anyone been to Mars?"

"Nope. Just the Moon, and we haven't even been back there since the seventies."

I see. Mankind must have decided to put their effort and resources into transforming the Earth into a paradise. No war, hunger, disease...

I laughed, but immediately felt horrible about it. "I'd say that things aren't that different from the world you remember. In fact, in a lot of ways, things are worse."

How is this possible? I spent my entire life showing humanity it's potential, the wonders it could accomplish if only we tried..."

"Yeah, that's exactly it. Nobody tries. They're all squabbling over a bigger slice of the pie and nobody gives a rat's ass about anyone else."

Walt was silent for a long time. The colors swirling on the screen were dark and somber.

"Is there no hope?"

"There's always hope. Lots of folks still dream like you did, it's just that the reality of the human race makes it really hard to get anything done."

"I think I understand." The sadness in his voice was palpable.

"I'm sorry if I've got nothing but bad news." I glanced at my watch. "Look, I have to go for a while. I'll be back after my last class."

"Yes, of course. Goodbye."

I switched off the receiver, and left the room to its still darkness.

* * *

It was impossible to concentrate in class, I just sat through it like a zombie, staring vaguely in the direction of the chalkboard until the time ran out and we were released.

I thought about bringing Campbell down to the pit and showing Walt to him, but somehow I was certain that he'd only make a mockery of it. Still, I wanted to show *someone,* and it suddenly dawned on me that I could be recording my conversations with the ghost. I ran to my car and dug out the old VCR I'd been using for class projects, and sprinted down to the pit.

Luckily, the monitor jacks out of the receiver were straight RCA plugs, so it was easy to feed the signal into the VCR and pass that through to the monitor. I switched everything on, but while the picture looked as trippy as ever, there was no audio.

"Hello, Walt?"

"Hello Michael."

"Ah, you scared me for a minute there. I thought you were gone."

"No, I'm here. I was just thinking."

"Oh really? What about?"

"This is wrong, Michael."

"What? What's wrong?"

"Me. The fact that I am trapped here in this limbo."

"I thought that was temporary. Isn't the whole idea behind being frozen to wait until the day that they can fix what's wrong with you and bring you back to life?"

"Yes, that was the general plan. But it's not working like I thought it would."

"What do you mean?"

"For one thing, I thought I'd sleep until they woke me. Instead, I've spent forty years alone in the darkness, fighting for my sanity."

I could see how that might suck. "But you aren't alone any more!"

"In some ways, that's even worse. You've shown me the error of my thinking."

"I don't get it."

"I wanted to awaken in the future – my future – shiny and new, happy and healthy, clean and full of promise. It never really occurred to me that the world wouldn't rise above its problems."

"Hey, we're working on it! Things are getting better, just more slowly than you thought. They say people will be going to Mars sometime in the next twenty years, people are still working for world peace, science is making new breakthroughs every day…"

"How much longer do I need to wait? Has cancer been cured?"

"Uh, no, not yet, but they are making progress…"

"I can't go on like this. Talking to you has helped, but it's still difficult to believe that you are real. Your voice sounds suspiciously just like my own, and I can't even point in the direction it is coming from. I can't see anything and I can't feel anything but this god-forsaken cold.

"There are others you could talk to! Hell, if this went public, I bet you could be a big star again! People would pay big money to talk to Walt Disney's frozen head."

"No, Michael. That's not what I want. This is unnatural. It was pure hubris to think I could circumvent God's will and live more than my allotted time on Earth. This has to end."

I was stunned. "What do you mean? You want to die?"

"I am already dead. I died over forty years ago. The only reason my spirit has not moved on is that I am trapped in this purgatory of science."

"What... what do you want me to do about it?"

"You say that I am frozen."

"Yeah, I think so..."

"You have to release me, Michael. I am begging you to end this."

* * *

I watched the VHS tape over and over. It was surreal, hearing only Walt's side of the conversation since it never occurred to me to mic myself, but I remembered my words just fine. I discussed the situation with Walt repeatedly in the following week, trying to talk him out of his resolve to die, but to no avail. In fact, in the end he convinced me that it was the right thing to do.

Now there was just the matter of actually doing it. Walt was behind a locked door, and I felt sure that walking around campus with a pair of bolt cutters would attract attention. I laid awake at night trying to think of ways to get into the freezer, but nothing seemed feasible. And what if I did get in? Would I even know how to disable whatever mechanism was keeping him conscious?

The answer came to me in a very unlikely place. I stumbled across a pile of empty 35 mm film cans in a back corner of one of the production studios, and snuck them out when no one was looking. Then it was just a matter of waiting.

I tried to keep Walt upbeat in the meantime, but he wasn't interested in talking much. He'd already resigned himself to oblivion, and maintaining contact with the living just seemed pointless. I explained my plan to him, but the best he could muster was that he thought I was "resourceful."

I was on campus earlier than usual on the 15th, since I had no idea what time I'd have to make my move. I chatted idly with Walt until I heard the jingling of keys.

"Well, this is it," I told him.

"Good luck."

"If this works, it's Goodbye."

"Yes."

"Last chance to change your mind."

Walt paused. *"No, this is what I want."*

I nodded. "OK then. Happy trails, Walt. The world is a poorer place without you."

"Thank you Michael. You've been a good friend."

I left the receiver on, picked up the stack of film cans and waited in the hall, praying that no one else came along.

I stood a few yards from the freezer door. It was open, the padlock hanging limply in the hasp, light and shuffling sounds coming from within. After what seemed like an eternity, the serviceman turned off the light and emerged. I ran towards him, trying to cover my face as much as possible with the tower of cans.

"Hold the door!! These have to go in there!"

Without a word, the man stood aside, holding the door for me. I pushed past him into the dark freezer, wisps of vapor curling in the air behind me like a ship's wake. I glanced around for the light switch and hit it with my elbow.

The inside of the freezer was largely empty, a few boxes stacked along one wall, several empty shelves ran the length of another. But my objective was obvious, a large stainless steel tank standing in one corner, connected by numerous pipes and hoses to a rack of liquid nitrogen cylinders.

"Hey, kid," shouted the man outside in the hall, "you gonna be long? I'm on a tight schedule."

"Right," I shouted back. "Yeah, this film stock has to be stored just right or it'll get ruined by frost. Go on ahead, I can lock it up."

I could hear the hesitation in his voice, but he clearly thought he'd just caught a break. "Thanks. Make sure you get it locked, or it's my ass."

"You got it!" I yelled, and I could hear him walking away. I held my breath until I was sure he was gone, then grabbed the padlock out of the hasp to make sure that no one could lock me in.

It was bitter cold, my breath as thick and visible as the plume from a steam train. I put the empty film cans down as quietly as I could and turned my attention to the tank. Somewhere inside was the frozen man I'd been talking to for what seemed like a very long time now. I wondered at why he was still conscious in there, how he was broadcasting his thoughts. I'd read somewhere that materials took on remarkable and strange properties when extremely cold. Perhaps somehow the electronics of this modern sarcophagus were interacting with his crystalline brain in a way that transmitted the weak signals.

However it worked, my purpose there was to make it stop. There didn't seem to be any kind of power switch on the tank, just the nitrogen hoses and a heavy electrical cord plugged into a 220 volt outlet on the wall of the freezer. That seemed to be the obvious choice, but I was terrified of being electrocuted while disconnecting the frost-covered plug. I gritted my teeth and touched it quickly and lightly, felt nothing, so I took a deep breath, grabbed the plug, turned it and pulled. It came away fairly easily. I half expected an alarm to go off, but nothing happened except that a barely audible hum stopped.

Next, I closed the valves on the nitrogen cylinders, but they were so cold that my hands nearly stuck to them. I thought about disconnecting the hoses, but it looked like that would require a wrench.

My work done, I reached to turn off the light, but stopped when I noticed the freezer's thermostat next to the switch on the wall. I turned it up as far as it would go, and turned off the power switch. Then I slapped off the light and hurried out of the freezer.

The hallway seemed positively balmy after the biting cold. I glanced around to make sure I was still alone, and locked the door – not with the padlock the service man had left, but one I had brought myself. I was guessing that no one would even try to get into the freezer until the service guy came back the following month, but the new lock would slow anyone down, as well as giving me a chance at getting back in should it be necessary.

My heart was ringing in my ears as I closed the door to the pit behind me, my breathing so fast that I was feeling dizzy. *It was done.*

Or was it? Tentatively, I approached the receiver. "Walt?"

There was no reply, no swirling colors on the monitor, just static. I played around with the antenna, adjusted the frequency, but there was no question about it, he was gone.

I worried that perhaps I had just shut off his means of communication, leaving him trapped and alone in the frozen darkness, as before. Even if that was the case, it was only a matter of time. With the power turned off, the slab of meat that had once been a man would slowly thaw, decay would set in, and then no miracle of science would be able to revive him. At long last, Walt Disney was beyond the future's reach.

* * *

I knew that my time at CalArts was at an end. I was no longer interested in pursuing a career in video; the world of entertainment now had a bitter aftertaste.

I spent the next year wandering aimlessly around L.A., working dead end jobs and drinking constantly to try and quiet my own mind. At night I was haunted by dreams of being embedded in ice, of being dug out by sinister robots and bug-eyed monsters whose only interest in me was as food.

I tried to tell a few trusted friends about Walt, but they didn't believe me, not even when I showed them the peculiar videotape of the one-sided conversation with a man who longed for death. They thought it was just a school project I'd done at CalArts, and weren't quite sure what to make of it.

One summer night in La Jolla, I couldn't sleep, so I went for a walk on the beach. The air was warm and humid, and the sky was clear and sharp. One star in particular sat near the horizon, sparkling like a diamond. I stared at it until it left a dark after-image when I looked away, a tiny dead spot in my visual field. I realized that dot was the perfect metaphor for Walt, and that the black hole I felt where he had been was fading over time, and that soon, it would be gone.

A dark, oppressive heaviness lifted from me. Walt may have been disappointed by the future that had so selfishly failed to live up to his expectations, but at that moment, I realized that *my* future would be of my own making. I wished for luck on the star, and kicked off my shoes.